THE MERCY KILLINGS

by

Geoff Collins

This book is a work of fiction. Names, characters, places and incidents are either the product of the author's imagination or are used fictitiously. Any resemblance to actual persons, living or dead, or to actual events or locales is entirely coincidental.

THE MERCY KILLINGS

Front cover art and cover designed by Erik Johnson
www.robertlangestudios.com/erik-johnson/

Back cover art:
Copyright © iStockphoto/469355564/Pureradiancephoto

Skull image:
https://pixabay.com/en/background-scrapbooking-paper-2079499/

Edited by Joe Gartrell and Ben Gibson of Word Mule.
www.wordmule.com

Published by A & J Publishing, LLC
3266 Hartwell
Johns Island, SC 29455

Visit the author website: www.booksbycollins.com

Categories: FICTION/Thrillers Crime

ISBN: 978-1-948046-07-7 (eBook),
ISBN: 978-1-948046-08-4 (paperback)

Version 2018.04.04

For...
Max, Leigh, and KC

A special thanks to Joe Gartrell and Ben Gibson of Word Mule.
www.wordmule.com

&

Erik Johnson
www.robertlangestudios.com/erik-johnson/

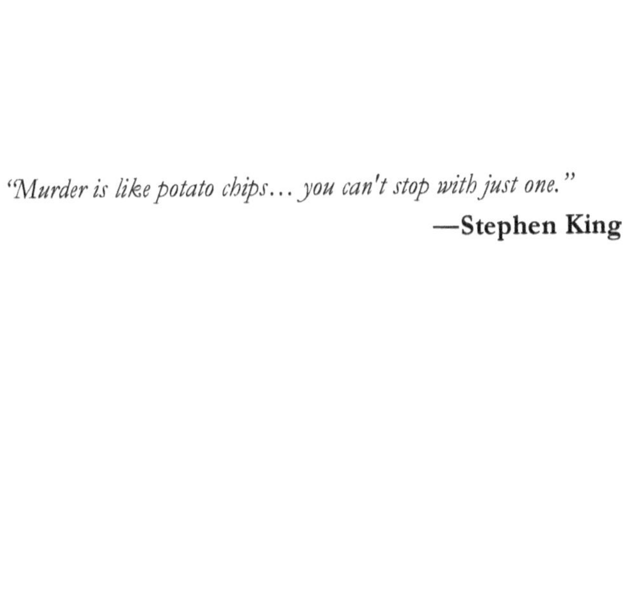

"Murder is like potato chips… you can't stop with just one."

—Stephen King

THE MERCY KILLINGS

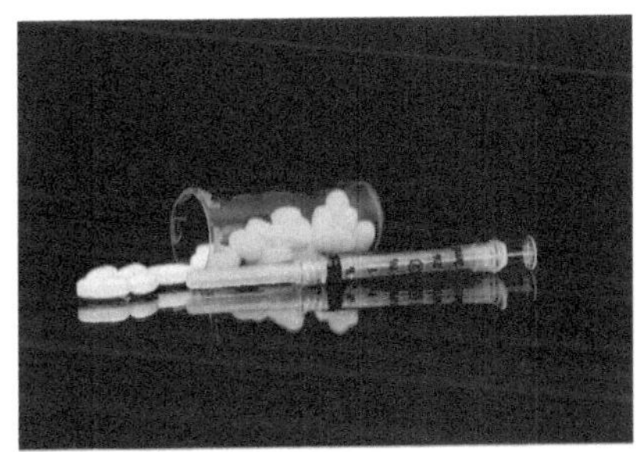

PROLOGUE

North Charleston, SC...2010

A LIGHT DRIZZLE spawned a golden-hued glow on the sidewalk under the halo of the streetlamp. The tree limbs bent low as if laboring under the weight of the thick night air. There was a sickening decay about the neighborhood, the smell of garbage and emptiness. A thin veil of dew lay on the windows of Nick's squad car affording him a somewhat ghostly view of the house. His shirt stuck to his back as he shifted weight in the front seat of the unmarked 2004 Crown Vic and glanced at his watch. 2:00 a.m.

Nick Giordano had been a North Charleston police officer for the past seven years, the last four spent with the department's K-9 Unit. It was only the second week of his assignment to the city's new drug task force—code-named *Street Sweeper*—but the late-night hours, stale coffee, and general tedium of surveillance were starting to grind on him. He had been parked a block from the corner of Remount and Murry watching the small house with its overgrown bushes and weed-covered lawn since about 11:00 that night. The corner house was not believed to be a trap house but rather a location from which a larger drop was being divided for distribution to drug parlors throughout the city. The house had been quiet all night, with no one entering or leaving. Nick's German Shepherd, Max, sat attentively in the backseat of the squad car. Nick turned around, ruffled his dog's ears, and said, "We'll give it another fifteen minutes, Max."

The task force was spread thin that night with multiple stakeouts throughout the known areas of drug activity in North Charleston. In the so-called "War on Drugs," police departments received federal grants based on total arrests rather than a declining crime rate. The department, like many across the country, was playing the numbers game. That this approach simply clogged an already overloaded court system and did little to stem the flow of drugs didn't seem to bother the suits in Washington. They measured the amount of drugs seized, but not whether arrestees were screened for drug addiction. They tallied the number of cases prosecuted, but not whether prosecutors reduced the number of petty crime offenders sent to prison. Despite all this, most police departments were underfunded and understaffed and had little choice other than bow to the demands of the politicians we all elected.

This was the third night Nick and his dog spent watching the corner house waiting for Luis Ramirez to show. Ramirez was one of a few upper-level distributors working directly with what was left of the Beltran-Leyva Cartel. While the once-prominent cartel had lost much of its power, it still controlled a major portion of the drugs coming into the greater Charleston area, as well as a handful of other U.S. cities. A `reliable informant indicated that Ramirez had recently been seen visiting the house on multiple occasions.

Nick had just finished off the last of his coffee and was about to call it a night when a black Dodge Charger, headlights turned off, pulled up and quietly rolled to a stop just beyond the house. A hooded man Nick assumed to be Ramirez exited the Charger carrying a large satchel and walked toward the house. Nick grabbed his binoculars and while he couldn't see the man's face, the guy matched Ramirez's physical description. "Max, looks like our boy showed up after all."

Nick called in a Code 8 requesting cover and back-up (no siren/no lights), clipped his control leash to Max's collar, slipped out of the Crown Vic, and remained low behind it. While waiting for backup, a light appeared behind closed shades in a room around the side of the house that Nick assumed to be a bedroom. After a few minutes, another police car appeared on the scene and parked a block away from Nick's squad car. Nick smiled when his good friend Billy Freeman exited the car. Nick and Billy had gone through the Academy together and remained close.

Freeman quietly made his way to the Crown Vic and, crouching next to Nick, whispered, "What's up, Nick?"

Nick gestured to the corner house and said, "Looks like there's a drop going down at that house. Definitely a crack den, smack shack, shooting gallery—whatever you want to call it. We've got intel that makes this location one of Luis Ramirez's main distribution cribs, and a dude just entered the house that matches Ramirez's description. The house has been dark, and I've seen no other activity in or around the place for the last three hours. I say we take it down."

Nick, like several officers on the taskforce, had been issued a "no-knock warrant," which permitted him to enter the premises without prior warning. Even though he knew he should wait for additional backup, three straight nights of boredom and the excitement of the moment got the better of him, and he went ahead and called in the Code 966, indicating a drug bust was in progress. Nick drew his Glock 21 and headed toward the house with Max and Billy following close behind.

The officers quietly approached the front door, taking positions on either side of the entryway. Nick felt the familiar rush of adrenaline pounding through his body, as his breathing and heart rate increased and his senses heightened. He took a deep breath, trying to calm himself, then flipped off the safety on his Glock and removed the control leash from Max's collar. As a drug-sniffing dog, Max had been trained to give the "passive alert" of lying down on all fours when he discovered the scent of drugs. As soon as Nick reached the door, his dog caught the scent and immediately dropped. Nick gently tried the doorknob, but it wouldn't budge. He looked at Billy and shook his head. Freeman, an ex-linebacker for the South Carolina Gamecocks, was six-foot three and a solid 240. He gave Nick a hand signal indicating he would kick in the door and then follow them in. Freeman mouthed "one, two, three" then shattered the door with his first kick.

Max was instantly up on all fours and charged through the entry followed by Nick and Billy yelling, "Police! Police! Police!" The living room was small and lit only by a shaft of light coming from a partially opened bedroom door. There was no furniture in the living room except for a mattress on the floor pushed up against the far wall. On top of it lay curled the motionless body of a naked woman. Nick, seeing the bedroom door ajar, gave Billy a hand sign indicating he would clear the room and headed in, his Glock raised in a two-handed shooting position. The room was empty with the exception of a table that held a block of cocaine and a box of sandwich bags.

Then everything seemed to happen all at once.

Drawn by the scent of drugs, Max raced directly to the mattress followed by Billy who made a quick two-finger check for a pulse on the woman's neck and called out, "Got a live one here!" Nick made a quick scan the bedroom, and seeing no one, yelled, "Bedroom clear!" Assuming Ramirez left through the back door, Nick tore from the bedroom and ran through the kitchen to the rear exit. Just as he burst through the back door, he heard the unmistakable sound of three gunshots coming in rapid succession from inside the house. He whirled around only to see Billy Freeman on the floor, half his face blown away, and Max lying next to him.

"Son of a bitch!" Nick screamed and was in the living room a second later.

As soon as he rounded the corner, he saw the flash. The bullet entered his chest right below his left shoulder and spun him around. The spin became a tumble as a second bullet shattered his right knee. He was losing focus, but managed to get off two quick rounds in the direction of the shooter before his world turned black.

Three squad cars arrived minutes later—their blue and red lights creating a carnival of color. The officers quickly secured the perimeter and entered the house. It looked like a war zone. The sharp metallic smell of gunpowder hung in the air. The first officers on the scene had called in a "ten-double-zero," indicating "officer down, all patrols respond." Nick was unconscious, crimson rivers of blood flowing freely from his chest and knee. One of the officers checked Billy for a pulse, even though it was obvious he was dead. Max's lifeless body lay on the floor next to him. One of the shots Nick was able to get off found Ramirez's heart. He was dead before he hit the floor. The naked woman remained passed out on the mattress, oblivious to the death that surrounded her.

When the EMTs arrived, they quickly assessed the situation, making sure Nick's airway was clear and then addressed the chest wound by sealing it off so air wasn't sucked into his chest. After he was stabilized, Nick was transported to MUSC's Level 1 Trauma Center in downtown Charleston.

Nick opened his eyes and blinked several times, allowing his pupils to adjust to the bright overhead lights of the hospital corridor, as he was rolled to the operating room. He was confused until the sharp pain in his chest and knee slapped him back to reality.

"Billy?" he whispered.

He felt a hand on his forehead and heard muffled voices in the background. Then the darkness returned.

Nick was in the operating room for over four hours. The cartridges used by Ramirez were 38 Specials. The entry wound in the upper chest was minimal, but the expanding effect of the bullet caused substantial damage upon exiting his back. The damage to his right knee was far worse. The team of surgeons at the Trauma Center was able to save his leg, but the bullet had shattered bone, ligaments, and cartilage.

After surgery, Nick was in and out of consciousness in the ICU for the next several hours. He caught fleeting sounds and images, none of which made sense to him. Finally, he opened his eyes and saw Ed Merchant, captain of the drug task force, and Lieutenant Steve Williams, who headed up his K-9 unit. Their faces were somber. When Nick managed to whisper, "Billy?", both men simply shook their heads. "Max?"

Lieutenant Williams took Nick's hand. "I'm so sorry, Nick."

Nick Giordano shut his eyes. Then came the tears.

CHAPTER ONE

HE OPENED HIS eyes, heart pounding, shirt soaked with perspiration. The nightmares weren't as frequent as they'd been, but when they came, they came hard. Nick rolled his legs over the side of the bed, sat up, and realized he was still fully clothed. His head felt like he'd been hit by a sledge hammer. He covered his eyes from the harsh morning sun and noticed the half-empty bottle of scotch on the nightstand. He grabbed his watch. 6:30.

The last thing he remembered the night before was leaving the International Lounge on Dorchester Road.

Nick stumbled out of bed and made his way to the kitchen. He set the coffeemaker and headed to the bathroom where he turned the shower on hot and searched the medicine cabinet for aspirin or whatever. He stripped off his foul-smelling clothes and spent the next five minutes in the shower, hoping to wash away what memories he had of the night before. Five aspirin, a hot shower, and two cups of black coffee—each spiked with a healthy shot of whisky—helped Nick settle his demons and kick-start the day. He made the fifteen-minute drive to the North Charleston Police Station's Fraud Division on Rivers Road.

It had been almost a year. Almost a year since his lack of judgment led to the death of his friend and fellow officer, Billy Freeman, and Max; the only dog he'd ever worked with during his four years at the K-9 Unit. That night in North Charleston he had made mistakes that would have been unacceptable even for a rookie fresh from the Academy. He'd asked himself the same questions thousands of times: *"Why didn't he wait for back up? Why didn't he clear the closet?"*

Nick was placed on paid administrative leave during the two-month-long deadly force investigation. The "shooting board" finally determined the shooting to be "with policy," and after he was cleared by the department psychologist, Nick was free to return to duty. He could no longer handle the physical requirements of the K-9 Unit and was transferred to a desk job in the Fraud Division. While the department had deemed him ready, he was, in reality, far from emotionally prepared to handle the day-to-day grind of being back on the job, even relegated to a desk.

The damage to Nick's leg was so severe that two additional surgeries were required to virtually rebuild the entire knee. The prognosis for a physical recovery was good, but it was clear that Nick would never regain the full use of his leg. The pain was a constant reminder of the deaths he considered himself responsible for that night in North Charleston. During the first six months after the surgeries, the pain was intense, especially late at night and early in the morning. He could have opted for pain pills, but as a police officer, he'd witnessed too many lives cut short by opioids, and in a way, he felt like he deserved the pain.

Virtually every city has its "cop bars," where police officers congregate to let their hair down and trade stories. Smokey's on Rivers Road was one of those spots. You could most always find a group of North Charleston's finest relaxing after their shift change. Before the shooting, Nick would make a practice of stopping by Smokey's for a beer or two about once a week. Those visits stopped after the shooting, but the beers did not. He'd never been much of a drinker, but bottles of scotch and twelve-packs of beer soon began to empty themselves in a day or two, and he would often find himself closing the bars around his one-bedroom apartment on Dorchester Road. Pick your poison.

At first, the drinking helped ease the constant pain in his leg and smooth over the emotional anxiety building inside him. As the months passed, his reliance on those late-night forays into the world of shots and beers escalated, and his interactions with fellow officers decreased. He just couldn't crawl out of his guilt—he was in too deep. On occasion, he'd wake up in the morning unable to recall where he had been the night before. And more than once, he awoke to find himself in the bed of some bat-faced woman whose name escaped him.

The nightmares kept coming, too, and Nick began to call in sick on a far too regular basis—sometimes not even bothering to call when he didn't show. He had been issued two Letters of Reprimand from his department captain. He was losing control, and he knew it. A darkness as thick as pitch surrounded Nick—his mind throwing up memories he couldn't deal with.

Finally, in August of 2011, he came to terms with his downward spiral, realizing he could lose his life if he didn't make a change. Nick loved being a cop, but now it was eating him up. The booze and the guilt were tearing his world apart. He had thought he could somehow honor the memory of Billy Freeman by staying on the force, but it just wasn't working. He needed to get out. And he needed to get out now.

The following week, Nick submitted his formal resignation from the force, packed a bag, and made the two-hour drive up I-26 to his dad's peach farm in Killian, South Carolina. It was time to go home.

CHAPTER TWO

NICK LOOKED FORWARD to seeing his dad and hopefully finding that special kind of peace that comes from returning home after being gone a long time. Robert Giordano had run his small peach farm for the past forty years, the last ten without his wife, Gloria, who passed away in 2001 from breast cancer. Nick's dad had never been much of a talker, but you could clearly sense a subtle dignity and deep strength of character the moment you met him. In his thoughtful, patient way, Robert Giordano refused to judge his son. He was simply there for him. Nick needed that.

Every month or so for years, Nick made the two-hour drive to Killian to spend a weekend at the farm with his dad. Since the shooting, the frequency of those trips grew less and less, until they just stopped altogether. His dad knew all about Nick's physical and psychological anguish, but he wasn't prepared for what he saw that August afternoon when Nick arrived.

Growing up in Killian, Nick had always excelled in athletics at Westwood High School. At six-foot one and 190 pounds, he was the starting point guard for the Redhawk's basketball team and an all-conference pitcher for the baseball team. He'd remained active at the University of South Carolina, and the physical demands of the K-9 Unit had kept him in excellent shape throughout his twenties. However, the aftermath of the shooting and the ravages of alcohol had taken their toll. Nick was in bad shape.

It had been almost six months since Robert Giordano had seen his son. His once short cropped hair had grown longer and looked as if it hadn't been washed in days. Nick had dropped over twenty pounds, and his sunken cheeks, pallid skin, and the dark circles around his eyes were stark reminders of the depth of his depression. It hung on him like ragged clothes—like the stale smell of cigarettes.

Nick parked in front of the house and walked slowly to his dad. He didn't say a word. He didn't look up. When he got to the porch, Robert took him into his arms and held him for some time before saying, "Son, it's good to have you home again. Come on inside and let's get you settled."

The two-story, three-bedroom farmhouse with its familiar sights, smells, and sounds hadn't changed much since Nick left for college well over ten years before. It spoke of a simpler and safer time when he'd yet to fully experience the harsh realities of the outside world.

Nick sat on his bed and drank in his surroundings. Memories flooded back as the last rays of late afternoon sun slanted through the bedroom window, illuminating tiny dust particles that seemed to be floating in a sea of air. His eyes rested on the bookshelf filled with baseball and basketball trophies he had received growing up in Killian. On the wall hung framed photographs of Trapper and Scout, two of the dogs he'd grown up with on the farm. So much had happened in his life since he had left this room—the sanctuary of his youth.

Eventually, he reined in his emotions and joined his father in the kitchen, as he was finishing making a plate of scrambled eggs and hash browns—Nick's favorite.

"Coffee, Son? Black with sugar, if I remember right."

"Thanks, Dad."

Robert poured his son the coffee and said, "Ran into your old buddy, Tim Ryan, the other day. He just got promoted to Manager at Ferguson Feed and Seed. Told him you'd be spending some time at the farm, and he'd like to get together."

Nick stared into his coffee which he held with both hands and seemed not to have heard his dad.

Robert waited a moment and then said, "Son, can I get you anything else to go with your eggs?"

Nick looked up and said, "No thanks. I'm just not that hungry, Dad. Sorry. It's been a long day. Tired. I think I'll just lay down for a while if that's okay."

"No problem. You go ahead and get some rest. We'll talk later."

Nick left the table, his coffee and food untouched. Upstairs in his room he laid down in his bed and eventually fell into a fitful sleep.

A few hours later, Robert looked in on his son and found him fast asleep curled up in the fetal position. He gently covered him with a blanket and then sat quietly with him for the next hour. He seemed so small laying in his bed—almost childlike, as his father tried to read the lines on his face. Finally, he rearranged the cover, kissed his son on the forehead, and walked down the dark hallway to his own bedroom.

Robert was up with the sun, and after checking on Nick, who was still sleeping, he made himself a small breakfast before leaving the farmhouse to meet the migrant field workers he had hired for the season. Days were long and work intense during peach season, which ran from mid-July through September. Picking peaches in the unforgiving heat and humidity of the South Carolina summer was backbreaking work. Robert relied on two Mexican families who lived on his property during the season and put in ten-hour days bringing in the harvest. There always seemed to be a shortage of good pickers, but Robert paid well and was fortunate enough to have the same two families return for three years running. And he needed all the luck he could get.

It was becoming harder and harder for small farmers like him to make a go of it, and large "corporate farms" had only gotten bigger over the years. In 2011—as is true with much of the country's wealth—the vast majority of America's farmland was controlled by a small number of farms, the top ten percent accounting for more than seventy percent of cropland in the United States; the top 2.2 percent alone taking up more than a third.

During the late-morning lunch break, Robert hauled the morning harvest back to the farmhouse and loaded the bushels onto his truck to be delivered to the county farm co-operative later that afternoon. Before returning to the field, he checked on Nick and found him in the upstairs bathroom. He knocked lightly on the bathroom door. "Son, you okay in there?"

"I'll be fine, Dad." Nick's voice sounded strained. "Just not feelin' real good. Don't worry about me."

"I've got to get back to the field. You sure you're all right? Can I get you anything?"

"No, Dad. You go ahead. I'll see you later." Nick heard the wooden steps creak under his father's weight and the back door shut shortly thereafter. He remained curled on the bathroom floor sweating profusely. He spent most of the balance of the afternoon in his bed dealing with a protracted headache and bouts of nausea. He did, however, make it downstairs later in the afternoon for a bowl of tomato soup and some fresh air.

His dad returned from delivering the day's harvest of peaches to the co-op around 6:30 and found Nick at the kitchen table, a blanket draped over his thin shoulders. It was once again clear how much his son's depression had not only affected him mentally but also had taken a major toll on his physical health. He knew his son had turned to alcohol to mask his depression, but didn't know the level of his dependence. Whatever the case, he knew it was critical to keep him hydrated, so he prepared beef broth and waited patiently as Nick drank it. They sat quietly at the kitchen table, until Robert broke the silence. "I know you've had a tough go of it this past year, and it took courage for you to leave the department and come home. We're gonna take this one step at a time. No pressure. We'll get through this thing together."

The next seven or eight days were hard on Nick. He had difficulty keeping down what little food he could eat and spent much of the day resting in his room. Eventually, his body cleansed itself, and he was able to join his dad in the field, although he was still too weak to be of much help. However, over the next few weeks he began to regain a portion of his strength and stamina to the point where he could offer some help with the harvest. He hadn't been home for a harvest since he was 18, and it felt good to be in the field. Nick had pinned a calendar on the wall in his bedroom, and each night before he went to sleep, he'd put an "X" on that day—another twenty-four hours without taking a drink.

As the end of September approached, it became clear that this year's peach crop would be exceptional. A late-spring frost the year before had cost Robert almost half his normal harvest, and the success of this year's take would allow him to bring his bank loan current and pay off other debts he'd incurred. Such is the life of a farmer. Even with all the modern world's technological advances, a farmer's fortunes still ebb and flow with the weather and the seasons. On the last day of September, Robert had the two Mexican families to the farmhouse for a cookout to celebrate the harvest. That night, Nick had a celebration of his own; he placed the fiftieth "X" on his calendar.

During his time home, Nick and his dad didn't speak much about the shooting and everything that came after, but they both took strength from their time together.

Even though the hectic season was over, there still was plenty of work to do on the farm. It was time to catch up on those maintenance items that had been set aside because of the demands of the harvest and tend to the peach trees. They had to be pruned to ensure nutrients weren't wasted on excess foliage. Dead and diseased branches needed to be removed, too.

Nick fell into a comfortable routine, and his dad's two dogs, Trip and Tony, became his constant companions as he went about his work on the farm. A neighbor once inquired as to the particular breed of his dogs, and Nick replied, "They're Labutts."

"Never heard of that breed, son," said the neighbor.

Nick laughed and said, "Yep, they're a cross between a Lab and a mutt!"

Living on the farm by himself since Gloria had passed away, Robert had become quite a cook. It didn't take long for Nick to regain the twenty pounds he'd lost and then some. While his mobility was limited by his leg and shoulder, the constant demands of farm work had put him in great physical shape. But the psychological trauma hadn't relented. He was still dealing with feelings of guilt and inadequacy that had festered since the shooting.

Officers were supposed to be in control of their emotions and everything else. Like many who work in law enforcement, Nick had become an expert at hiding his emotions. He lived in a dangerous and demanding profession where he was taught to maintain a sense of control in dealing with his feelings. Nick, like many officers, declined to participate in the voluntary counseling services his department offered for those involved in shooting incidents. But as his health improved, he grew to realize that his drinking and self-destructive lifestyle after the shooting were symptoms of a much more deep-seated problem. He finally accepted that he probably needed some sort of professional help to understand and deal with the demons that remained buried within him. Even though he knew better, he still felt that admitting he needed help was a sign of weakness. He was hesitant to talk about it, but he finally broached the subject with his dad one evening after dinner.

"Dad, I got a call yesterday from my old boss, Steve Williams. He wanted to see how I was doing and let me know the rest of the guys in K-9 were asking about me."

Robert was taking the dinner plates to the sink and paused. "That was nice of him," he said. "I remember you always respected Steve."

"He's a good guy," Nick agreed. "The first few days after I woke up in the hospital, he took care of everything. I remember him stopping by to see me almost every day while I was in there and calling to check up on me after I got out. You know, he was a beat cop in Charleston before he qualified for K-9. He told me that he shot some dude who pulled a gun on him one night. Didn't kill him, but apparently Steve was messed up for a while. He said talking to a shrink helped him deal with it."

"It's not always easy for men to open up about their feelings, but I know it can help."

Nick looked at his father dubiously, trying to imagine him sharing his feelings in any way other than an especially expressive handshake.

Robert finished clearing the dishes and had poured two cups of coffee before returning to the kitchen table. "You were at the university when your mom got sick. She was a strong woman, but the cancer got her. It was god-awful to see her suffer. I know it sounds strange, but I felt I failed her, that I should've been able to protect her. It felt like my fault when she passed. The only thing that seemed to help was work. I'd put in fifteen or sixteen hours a day on the farm, but at night I'd still get that feeling that I let her down." Robert smiled and offered a somber laugh. "You know, the farm never looked better than it did back then, but I've ever felt worse."

"I'm sorry, Dad," Nick said. "I had no idea. I just figured you could handle anything."

"I'm not that strong. Well, I never told you, but I finally talked to Doc Mathews about it, and he set me up with a therapist in Columbia named Lucas Smart. I always thought that was a great name for a head doctor," Robert chuckled. "Anyway, it helped. I'm not saying it took all the pain away, just got me to a point where I could accept what happened without blaming myself. I'll never forget the first time I met with him. He told me the depression and guilt were like a mental toothache. He said he could give me some pills to dull the pain, but it would keep coming back. The pain and depression were only symptoms, and the decay would continue to grow until we got to the root of the problem and pulled it out."

"Are you saying I should see someone like Dr. Smart?"

"That's your decision, Son. I just want you to know that no one will think less of you if you choose that path. All I can tell you is that it helped me."

"Thanks, Dad. I'll think about it."

It took time, but Nick finally decided to do it. His dad contacted Dr. Smart who recommended one of his colleagues, Dr. Judy Bailey. Nick felt comfortable with Dr. Bailey right off the bat and began meeting with her every Friday. Despite his comfort level with the doctor, it took Nick many sessions before he was able to open up. He first learned to accept his drinking and destructive behavior as merely symptoms for a much more deep-seated problem. The devastating guilt he felt from the death of his fellow officer and friend Billy Freeman and his dog Max led him to question his own self-worth. It took months of therapy to peel back the layers of guilt until he was eventually able to forgive himself for what had happened the night of the shooting and continue the process of regaining control of his life.

CHAPTER THREE

THE YEAR WITH his dad back home in Killian did wonders for Nick. He still walked with a pronounced limp, and the nightmares had not completely disappeared, but he'd kicked the booze and was slowly becoming ready to shed the safety of the farm and move on with his life. But move on to where?

One night in late October, Robert asked Nick to take a walk with him. The intense heat of the summer had waned, and a pleasant breeze cooled the evening air. Stars littered the night sky, and a crescent moon cast a soft silver light across the seemingly endless rows of peach trees. Nick and his father walked in silence, both lost in thought.

About fifteen minutes in, Robert slowed and turned to Nick. "Son, I can't tell you how nice it's been having you here this last year, and you know you're welcome to stay as long as you want, but maybe it's time to think about what you want to do when you leave the farm. As much as I'd love having you stay, we both know you're not cut out for the farm life. You need to get back out in the world and do something you love."

"I know, Dad. I've been thinking about it, but I'm not sure what I want to do. Hell, I'm not even sure what I can do. All I've ever been is a cop." Nick was right. Before starting his career, he'd spent four years at the University of South Carolina getting his B.A. in Criminology. He had a sense of fulfillment during his time as a police officer. He felt he was making a real difference until the shooting ended it all. He still considered himself a cop, even though he knew that life would never be his again. Nick accepted that but just couldn't picture himself doing anything else.

"Listen, Son, just because your days on the force are over, it doesn't mean you lost the skills you learned there. You have a gift. I've seen it ever since you were a kid. You connect with dogs. You put that gift to work while you were with K-9, so why not put it to work again?"

The question caught Nick off guard. "What do you mean?"

"I mean have you ever thought about training dogs again? I'm not talking about sit, roll over, and beg—I'm talking about training police dogs. You know as well as anyone there's always a demand for professionally trained police dogs, and you certainly have the tools. What do you think?"

Nick didn't know what to say. It was true he'd had a kinship with dogs all his life. He couldn't remember a time when there weren't one or two dogs on the farm when he was growing up. And there was Max. For four years, Max was his constant companion. It was almost like they could read each other's minds. Despite the hell he'd gone through, he'd never lost his passion for law enforcement. He missed his "Blue Blood" brothers and sisters and that special bond that exists among those who serve together.

Robert smiled and said, "Now, I don't want you to be upset with me, but I've been having some conversations with Lieutenant

Williams, and he thinks it's a great idea. You wouldn't have to work for someone else. This would be your own business. He even said he'd be glad to do what he can to help."

"But I wouldn't even know where to start!" Nick said, still somewhat stunned.

"Slow down, Son, one step at a time. You told me the dogs your K-9 unit got were already trained. I checked into it. A lot of these dogs are trained in Europe, but the closest place that trains them in the States is in Georgia. The business paperwork is fairly simple, and Lieutenant Williams told me he knows a perfect three-acre piece of land out on Johns Island that's about to go up for auction."

"Dad, I appreciate all that," Nick said. "But there's no way I can possibly afford that land, build kennels, and get the equipment to make a go of it."

Nick's dad was quiet for some time. A cool breeze rustled through the peach trees. "Well," he finally said, "that's where your partner comes in. This last year with you has been good for me. It's just been me here since your Mom passed, and I've managed to put away a few dollars. I can't think of a better use for that money than helping get your life started again. So, if this is something you think you would really want to do, I'm willing to shake on it right now."

Robert extended his callused hand, and when Nick took it, his dad pulled him close and whispered, "Love you, Boy."

Maybe his dad was right. Maybe this could work. Maybe this was as close as he could get to being a cop again. Nick began to see his future taking shape—he felt hopeful for the first time in more than two years.

It was surprising how quickly everything unfolded. With the help of his dad and Lieutenant Williams, the land was bought, fencing installed, a dozen kennels constructed, necessary training equipment purchased, and the initial batch of German Shepherds delivered to the Academy within the first three and a half months.

On the last Saturday of 2012, Robert, Lieutenant Williams, and a handful of Nick's friends from the force joined him out on Johns Island for the official opening of the Low Country Police Dog Academy. It wasn't all smooth sailing. It rarely is. But with Nick's talent and hard work, along with a little help from his old boss, the demand for his dogs began to grow. Word spread quickly, and soon inquiries started coming in from K-9 departments in North Carolina and Georgia, in addition to South Carolina. By 2017, Low Country Police Dog Academy had four employees and a two-month backlog of orders for Nick Giordano-trained police dogs.

Nick had rented a 900 square-foot, one bedroom loft on Bee Street right next to the sprawling Medical University of South Carolina Hospital—the same hospital where he was rushed that fateful night.

There was a small coffee shop called "The Coffee Cup" next to Nick's place at the corner of Bee Street and Courtenay Drive. The shop, a mainstay in the area for years, was referred to as "The Cup" by its regular clientele. He soon got to know the owner, employees, and several of the other regular customers who frequented The Coffee Cup. As he had at the farm, Nick settled into a comfortable routine. If he grabbed his morning joe from The Coffee Cup by 7:30, he could time the traffic just right to be out on Johns Island by 8 o'clock.

CHAPTER FOUR

NICK WALKED INTO The Cup and was welcomed by a warm blanket of air carrying the rich aromas of fresh coffee and baked goods. Chestnut brown tables and soft leather chairs extended the same promise of comfort. The rhythmic hum of small talk blended with the whirring coffee grinder, the gurgling of coffee brewing, and the bubbling of the steamer warming the milk. The Coffee Cup, being smaller, had a much more "homey" feel to it than the more traditional Starbucks type coffee houses.

Nick smiled at the petite, dark-haired girl behind the counter and was about to order when she said, "Let me guess, Mr. Unpredictable, a blueberry muffin and coffee?"

"I think you just read my mind. Good morning, Amy. How's school treating you?"

"Keepin' me busy, Nick. That's for sure!"

Nick smiled at her, left a ten on the counter, and made his way to an open table with his coffee and blueberry muffin.

Amy Anderson lived in a small apartment on James Island and had worked at The Coffee Cup for the past six months. She'd gone through a painful, heart-wrenching divorce a year and a half earlier and, at thirty years old, was back in school at The University of Charleston chasing a degree in Elementary Education. Amy didn't talk much about the breakup, but Nick had heard it was bad. He felt a certain connection with her because they'd both had to reassemble a life from its broken pieces. They had grown to be good friends and had even met a few times for drinks. At about five foot three and a slim 115 pounds, Amy's long jet-black hair was highlighted by her clear, almond skin. She projected that simple kind of beauty, the kind that didn't require the assistance of much makeup. Her bright green eyes were filled with curiosity, and her smile could easily disarm the grumpiest of customers. She was definitely "easy on the eyes," and Nick had recently given some serious thought to the possibility of easing their relationship to the next level.

After a few minutes of checking his email, Nick heard a soft voice whisper, "Hey, mister, you gonna eat the rest of that muffin?"

Nick turned around to see the smiling face of Angela Martin dressed in her navy-blue scrubs. "Hey, Angela. Have a seat, but keep your hands off my muffin!"

Angela was one of several regulars who got their caffeine fix every morning at The Cup. She was an ER nurse at Mercy General, a good-sized hospital adjacent to MUSC. She grew up with her mom in North Charleston's Union Heights neighborhood, one of the toughest areas in the city. Like many single parents, her mom had worked multiple jobs to make ends meet. Despite the hardship, Angela managed to graduate from North Charleston High School with honors and eventually earned her registered nurse degree from Trident Community College in Charleston. Her hard work paid off when she hit thirty and was able to purchase a small home in one of North Charleston's nicer neighborhoods and move her mom in with her. For thirty years, Angela's mom had given her a safe and loving home—now it was her turn to return the favor.

"How's the dog business, Nick?" Angela asked as she slid into a seat next to him.

"It's all good, Angela. How's your mom settling in?"

"Oh, she misses some of the old gang in Union Heights, but she's adjusting." Angela chuckled, "I think she's getting used to a shower with dependable water pressure and air conditioning that actually works!"

They chatted for another ten minutes or so before Nick made the short walk to his condo's parking garage and drove out to Johns Island in his 2013 Toyota truck, arriving at the Academy at about 8:20.

He opened the security gate and pulled into the parking lot next to the used mobile home trailer that had been modified to act as his company's office. The grounds of the Academy were laid out in a simple but efficient way. Off to the left were the kennels consisting of twelve individual units for the German Shepherds. Behind the office, and covering the majority of the facility, was the actual training area. It was an open field of freshly mowed grass covered with a variety of wooden hoops, ladders, ramps, and jumps used to create obstacle courses for the dogs. There was a storage shed and another small building near the back of the property. The office, kennels, and training facility were surrounded by an eight-foot high chainlink fence topped with four rows of forty-five degree barb wire. The fencing was required by the insurance company, but considering a sale price of $12,000 to $15,000 for a fully trained police dog, it was more than worth the investment.

Sally Reed, Nick's gray-haired, slightly portly office manager, was on the phone and waved good morning to Nick when he walked into the trailer. He didn't know what he'd do without Sally. Luckily, he'd been able to convince her to join his fledgling company after she retired from a twenty-five year career as office manager for the Johns Island Police Department. Sally handled purchasing, invoicing, payroll, taxes, and just about everything else, with the exception of actually training the dogs. She was protective of Nick and never having children of her own, treated him almost as if he was her son.

After an hour of answering messages and shuffling papers, Nick headed outside to the training area to check on the dogs. He shared the training responsibility with Josh Taylor who'd been a sergeant in the Army's K-9 Unit with multiple tours in Iraq and Afghanistan before a disability discharge ended his active days in the service. Josh had been with the company since shortly after it started back in late 2012 and, like Nick, had received his Master Trainer Certification from the National Tactical Police Dog Association (NTPDA). Taylor was only five foot nine but carried a solid 180. He'd maintained his military haircut and preferred to wear his camouflaged cargo pants and high-laced combat boots. He was definitely Army through and through. Despite his small stature, he was the kind of guy you'd want next to you, whether it was in a firefight in Afghanistan or a bar fight in North Charleston.

"Morning, Josh. What've we got going today?" Nick asked.

"Hey, Nick. Working with Champ and Bandit this morning. Gonna spend some time with Bullet this afternoon. I think Champ and Bandit are both just about ready for their Narcotic Detection Certification test. I'd say it's safe to schedule it."

"Great. I've been getting calls from Atlanta asking when they can have their dogs." It wasn't even 10:00 yet, but you could already feel the oppressive heat and humidity coming on. "I want you to go easy on them today. It's headed for the high nineties. It's gonna feel like a sauna this afternoon," Nick added as he headed toward the kennels to check on the rest of the dogs. Temperatures and humidity in South Carolina summers could be brutal, especially for the dogs.

Nick thought how far Josh had come since he joined the company back in early 2013. Hundreds of combat missions during his three tours in Iraq and Afghanistan had taken a toll on him, physically and mentally. In 2011, Josh and his bomb-sniffing dog, Rocky, were working with a Marine task force in southern Afghanistan's Kandahar Province when an IED killed Rocky and seriously injured him. He eventually recovered from his physical injuries; however, the accumulation of stress from his three years of missions, culminating in the loss of Rocky, led to his disability discharge from the service.

Like many men and women returning home from combat, Josh found it difficult to adjust to civilian life and suffered from severe bouts of PTSD. He felt stuck in a perpetual nightmare and found it almost impossible to handle even the simplest of social interactions. In early 2013, one of Josh's counselors from the VA saw Nick's advertisement for "a canine trainer with experience training police or military dogs." The counselor contacted Nick, and after explaining Josh's history, he decided to take a look at him. Nick felt a connection—they'd both been scarred by the loss of their dog and career in a traumatic incident.

When Josh showed up at Nick's office, he was clearly ill at ease. He could barely make eye contact with Nick and was reluctant to talk about his time in the service. The interview was a disaster, but when Josh started to interact with the dogs, he seemed to calm down—so did the dogs. It was quickly apparent that Josh Taylor knew what he was doing. Nick hired him on the spot. It was a slow process, but as time passed, Josh learned to deal with his disability and became not only an important part of the business but also a good friend.

As Nick approached the kennels, he had to smile when he heard the high-pitched voice of Isaiah Robinson. "Sweet Jesus, you dogs sure do know how to make a mess!"

Isaiah, more commonly referred to as "Old Man Robinson," was a fixture around Johns Island for as long as anyone could remember. No one seemed to know just how old "Old Man Robinson" was, and he seemed to delight in that. When asked his age, he'd simply reply, "Don't rightly know myself."

Nick gauged Isaiah to be in his late eighties, if not older. His weathered face carried a perpetual smile, even though the majority of his teeth had departed decades ago. Nick often wondered what Isaiah's life must have been like growing up in the heyday of racial injustice in the South. These days, Charleston was definitely one of the more progressive southern cities, but all it took was a pickup truck with a rebel license plate or someone flying a confederate flag to remind you that some level of prejudice seethed just below the surface.

Isaiah lived by himself in a small trailer about a mile or so down the road from the Academy. A few years back, he started showing up around the kennels to watch Nick and Josh work with the dogs. He'd ride up on his bike, which looked to be about half as old as he was. Nick got to know Isaiah and eventually offered him a part-time job cleaning out the kennels and feeding the dogs.

"Good morning, Isaiah," Nick said.

"Mornin' to you, Mr. Nick. Sure be a hot one today. I gonna put some extra water out for my dogs 'for I leave."

"That's a good idea, Isaiah. Don't forget to turn on those fans before you go."

"Will do, Boss."

Nick spent the rest of the morning working with the dogs, consulting with Josh, and charting the progress of the twelve German Shepherds that were currently in training at the Academy. By two o'clock, the temperature was creeping close to one hundred degrees, and Nick shut down any further training.

CHAPTER FIVE

"YOU WON'T HEAR from me again until I complete the assignment and submit my written report to Mr. Rennells in Chicago," said Allen Miller.

"So, let me get this straight," barked Blake Fitzgerald, Chief Security Officer at Mercy General Hospital, "you're planning to hack into our security systems, mess around with our firewalls, and extract confidential data."

"First of all," Allen replied with little if any emotion, "I don't 'mess around' with any aspect of your cybersecurity system, and no confidential data will be taken. I simply identify whether your patients' confidential information is subject to a breach and, if so, suggest solutions. Plus, my fee is due only if I can identify specific areas where I could, if I chose to, compromise your system.

"I'm sure you're aware that hospitals and the healthcare industry are now the number one target of cybercriminals. It's no longer the banks, businesses, or the government. IBM predicts that one in every thirteen patient's medical records will be hacked within the next five years."

Fitzgerald, while known to be a technically competent executive, had a reputation of being somewhat egocentric and difficult to work with. "I'm very familiar with the threat facing our industry," he said, "and I'm also very confident in the ability of my people to deal with that threat."

Charles Summerton, Mercy General Vice President, stood and said, "I wouldn't worry, Blake. Mr. Miller comes highly recommended, and what we learn here can be applied to the rest of MediGroup's hospitals and medical facilities across the country. Plus, Rennells made it clear that he specifically wanted Mr. Miller to analyze our cybersecurity operations and make sure our patient data is secure.

"Mr. Miller, as I understand it, no one here at Mercy, including Mr. Fitzgerald and myself, will have any contact with you whatsoever during your analysis, and you will not be allowed on company property. Correct?"

"Correct," replied Allen. "My final report will go directly to Mr. Rennells, and I'm sure he will share the results with both of you. I will also need your assurances that no one outside the two of you will have any knowledge of the project, with the obvious exception of Mr. Rennells in Chicago."

"Understood," said Summerton. "Welcome aboard and happy hunting, so to speak." Summerton slid a letter across his desk and asked Allen to review and sign it. "It simply outlines our standard nondisclosure agreement."

Allen read the document, signed it, and slid it back across the desk. Mr. Summerton shook Allen's hand and said, "Good luck, sir."

As soon as Allen shut the door on his way out of Summerton's office, Fitzgerald shook his head and said, "I don't like this, Chuck. My team is good. Plus, we've got no control over what this guy does. For God's sake, he looks like he's still in college. He comes into our offices wearing a sport coat and a pair of blue jeans. And Christ, Chuck, he's got a ponytail! What the hell makes him so special?"

Summerton sat back down behind his desk, looked directly at Fitzgerald, and in no uncertain terms, said, "Take it easy, Blake. I've been told Mr. Miller has quite a reputation, and this directive comes straight from Rennells, so there's not much we can do about it. But even though I said we'd be the only ones who know what he's doing, I say we advise Jerry Shields. He's your main cyberguy, right?"

"Yeah, and he's good. That makes sense. I have no doubt he'd notice someone messing with the system, anyway."

"Can we trust Shields to keep this quiet?"

"Absolutely. If I tell him to keep his mouth shut, he will."

Summerton thought for a moment and said, "Go ahead and tell him we're running a test on the security of our patient's data, but impress the importance of keeping this under wraps. If he's got any concerns, he can come directly to me. Nobody else is to know about the project. Understood?"

"All right, I'll tell him," Fitzgerald said, feeling somewhat more in control of the situation now having one of his people involved.

Summerton stood and said, "Now, it's business as usual, and that means you're five minutes late for your staff meeting."

Fitzgerald, still obviously uncomfortable with the situation, looked at his watch and muttered, "Shit! All right, but remember it's my ass on the line, too."

As soon as Fitzgerald left the office, Summerton called Jack Rennells' private phone number in Chicago.

Rennells answered on the first ring. "Yes?"

"Mr. Miller signed the agreement and just left my office."

"Thank you, Charles."

Jack Rennells hung up and remained seated for some time before removing a key ring from his pocket and opening a locked desk drawer. He removed a manila folder with "Allen Miller" printed on the cover and "Secret Clearance-Alpha" stamped in red ink.

CHAPTER SIX

THERE ARE THREE basic secret clearance classifications for government and government-authorized personnel. The lowest level is "Confidential Clearance." It covers information that reasonably could be expected to *cause damage* to national security if disclosed to unauthorized sources. The vast majority of military personnel and congressional staff are given this basic level of clearance.

The second highest is "Secret Clearance" and covers information that reasonably could be expected to *cause serious damage* to national security if disclosed. This classification is normally given to specific elected government officials and to mid-level personnel in the CIA, NSA, and DHS.

"Top Secret" is our country's highest recognized security clearance and deals with information that could *cause exceptionally grave damage* to national security. Obviously, this classification is reserved for a relatively small number of top-level military and governmental officials.

Each of these classifications has a variety of subcategories. Allen Miller's classification was "Secret Clearance-Alpha," one step under "Top Secret."

The dossier that Jack Rennells held in front of him was highly redacted, but enough information could be drawn for a fairly good overview of Miller's history and cyber-related capabilities. Years of cultivating contacts in Washington allowed Rennells to take advantage of certain governmental back channels, which are much more prevalent than you'd expect. Favors given equal favors taken.

Allen Samuel Miller was born in Charleston, South Carolina in 1987. His parents, Julius and Elizabeth Miller, were fixtures in Charleston society. For years, Julius headed up the Commercial and Investment Banking business for J.P. Morgan's Charleston operations, and Elizabeth sat on a variety of boards at the heart of Charleston's social scene. Needless to say, Julius and Elizabeth Miller were an integral part of what you might call the "Charleston Elite."

Allen attended the prestigious Charleston Collegiate School which was located just outside of Charleston proper and catered to those Charleston families that could afford the sky-high tuition. The budget could have been mistaken for a small college. While the curriculum at the school was one of the most challenging in the country, Allen found the content lacking, with the exception of his computer classes. By his freshman year in school, Allen was writing code, developing his own software programs, and starting to experiment with hacking into local companies and government offices. He considered himself a "white hat" hacker and never had any intention of stealing information or harming whoever or whatever he chose to hack. He simply enjoyed finding "holes" in systems and relished the challenge of solving problems.

Before long, his computer teacher accepted the fact that he could no longer effectively challenge Allen and, with the help of Allen's father, arranged for him to sit in on some advanced computer classes at the University of Charleston. During his senior year, colleges and universities across the country were lining up to lure Allen Miller to their campuses. The Massachusetts Institute of Technology (MIT) finally won the battle, and Allen was off to Cambridge to study computer science and engineering. Through an accelerated program, he was able to complete both his undergraduate degree in computer science and engineering and his MS in cybersecurity in less than four years. Allen loved his years at MIT, where he could interact with some of the most talented technological minds in the world.

Despite the gloomy employment market when he graduated in 2009, Allen had lucrative job offers from virtually all the top tech companies. He surprisingly opted for a government job with the United States Computer Readiness Team (US-CERT) based in Washington, DC. US-CERT is an elite team of computer professionals within the Department of Homeland Security charged with protecting the nation's Internet infrastructure by coordinating defenses against and responses to cyberattacks. By the time Allen left his job at US-CERT in late 2016, he was considered one of the top cybersecurity experts in Homeland Security. But his reputation was not limited to government circles. Corporate America was taking notice, too.

Allen returned to Charleston after he left the government to found CyberNet Security, Inc. He rented a small nondescript second-floor downtown office on Queen Street, a little less than two miles from his recently purchased three-bedroom Bee Street condominium. The office space itself may have been less than impressive; however, he spent a small fortune on the latest cybersecurity computer systems. The only other employee of CyberNet Security was his secretary/assistant, Sarah Pryor.

Sarah had taught computer classes in a local high school for the last five years until she called it quits. She loved working with the kids, but felt smothered by the mountain of school district rules and regulations that dictated what and how to teach her students. It's no wonder over one-third of new teachers leave the public-school system within the first five years of teaching. Sarah lived downtown with her husband, Dave, who taught undergraduate history at the University of Charleston, and she had just started taking some graduate-level computer science classes at night at the University of Charleston. Allen was lucky to have Sarah. She was not only an efficient secretary but also displayed a good working understanding of the basic technology of cybersecurity.

From the beginning, CyberNet Security had no problems finding clients, and Allen was quite selective in which companies and individuals he chose to work with.

CHAPTER SEVEN

A WEEK BEFORE Allen's meeting with Summerton and Fitzgerald at Mercy General, he joined his dad for lunch at the prestigious downtown Charleston Harbour Club—strictly white linen tablecloths, Oneida silverware, and waiters in red jackets.

"Son, it's good to see you. Tell me how the world's treating you."

"The world is treating me fine, Dad. The decorators are just about finished updating my new condo, and I'm working on getting it furnished. How about you and Mom?"

"We're good. Off to our place in Belize with some friends next week. Don't forget, it's there whenever you want to use it."

"Thanks, Dad. I appreciate the offer."

"How's your latest cyber puzzle going?"

"It's been a pretty demanding problem, but I think we're going to wrap it up soon. What's your favorite line about how problems are like washing machines?"

His father grinned and said, "They twist, they spin, and knock us around. But in the end, we come out cleaner, brighter, and better than before."

Allen laughed, "Well, let's just say I'm in the final spin cycle."

Drinks were ordered and after a respectable amount of additional small talk, Julius set his scotch aside and said, "Son, I received a call from Jack Rennells at MediGroup up in Chicago the other day. You've met him a few times when he's visited your mother and me here in Charleston."

Allen smiled. "I remember him, Dad, and I'm assuming you're mentioning this because he wants something."

Julius laughed. "And so he does, and so he does. Jack's the CEO of MediGroup, a holding company for a slew of hospitals and other medical facilities."

"Yes, I'm somewhat familiar with the company."

"Good. So, he wanted me to talk to you about the possibility of doing some work for him."

"Great," Allen said. "Just have him give me a call."

Julius was quiet a moment before continuing. "Look, Allen. I'm not sure exactly what Jack needs done, but he made it perfectly clear that whatever it is, he needs it done 'under the radar.' He'd like to fly into Charleston later this week and meet with you at our house."

A request for secrecy was not at all unusual in Allen's business. Much of his cybersecurity work was done with relative anonymity.

"That's fine, Dad. Just let me know when he wants to meet, and I'll be there."

~~~~
~~~~

Allen's meeting with Mr. Rennells was set for Friday afternoon at the Miller's home on Church Street in downtown Charleston. MediGroup's private plane landed at the Charleston Executive Airport where a limo and driver were waiting. The twenty-five-minute drive to downtown Charleston had Jack at the Miller's house shortly after 1:00.

The house was less than a ten-minute walk from Allen's Queen Street office, and when he arrived at 2:00 sharp, he found Rennells and his parents waiting for him in the living room. Rennells stood and extended his hand to Allen. "It's good to see you, Allen," he said. "You look great."

"Thank you, sir. It's a pleasure to see you again. It's been a while."

"That it has, Allen." Rennells turned to Allen's parents and nodded. They got the hint.

Elizabeth smiled and said, "You two go right ahead and talk. Use the library. Can I get you something to drink, Allen?"

"No thanks, Mom, I'm fine." Jack picked up his briefcase and followed Allen down the hallway to the large oak-paneled library. Allen quietly shut the door.

Rennells' personality reminded Allen of the senior level military officers he'd dealt with while at CERT. High level leaders, corporate and military, tended not to waste time with ancillary conversation, giving the impression that other important matters were waiting in the wings. It was a display of confidence and comfort with their authority.

After they were seated, Jack began, "Allen, I want to thank you for seeing me today. I appreciate it. I'm needed back in Chicago so let me get right to it. I've followed your accomplishments over the years, especially your work at Homeland Security. I have a situation that requires not only someone with exceptional computer expertise, but someone I can trust implicitly with very sensitive information. And I'd like to believe you're that someone. So, whether or not we take this further, I do need your promise that what I'm about to tell you will remain confidential."

"You have my word," Allen answered without hesitation.

"All right. A few weeks ago, I received a call from Charles Summerton, our V.P. in charge of Mercy General Hospital here in Charleston. He told me his accounting manager, Russ Slean, was concerned with the gross margin numbers in the hospital's pharmacy department. Like many hospitals, Mercy General has been under increased pressure to cut costs, and about six months ago, they hired an outside pharmacy management company named PharmaTech to replace its in-house department. Shortly after the change, Russ noticed the pharmacy's margin performance began slipping four to five percent below previous levels. This made no sense because patient levels had remained relatively constant. He started quietly looking into the matter.

"Not long after PharmaTech was hired, there was an increase in turnover in the hospital's shipping and receiving department, and about a month ago, its manager, Chuck Thompson, unexpectedly submitted his resignation. During his exit interview, he was asked why he had decided to leave Mercy. Thompson would give no specific reason other than he needed to deal with a family matter.

"Shortly after Slean began monitoring the pharmacy's margins, he had a few confidential meetings with the hospital's purchasing manager, Chris Davis, to see if they could figure out what was really going on. Soon after that, Davis's health began to deteriorate to the point where he was forced to take a leave of absence.

"This further heightened Slean's belief that there may be a problem with the hospital's narcotics inventory control procedures. After several months of margins remaining at the depressed level, he brought his concerns to Charles Summerton. Apparently, Mr. Slean wanted to contact corporate accounting with his concerns, but Summerton wisely said he would handle the matter directly with me, and that's when Summerton contacted me.

"I need to find out what's going on and if there's a security problem with narcotics at Mercy deal with it. My concern is that any internal investigation runs the risk of alerting whoever might be involved. I need someone from outside to covertly probe the situation without raising red flags."

"Have you considered contacting the police?"

"We discussed that; however, we have nothing incriminating to give the authorities, and their presence would undoubtedly tip off whoever might be involved."

Allen nodded and said, "I can appreciate your problem."

"Also, as CEO, I need to put some distance between this situation and myself. While I'm ultimately responsible for what happens at MediGroup's individual companies, I do have a fiduciary responsibility to our shareholders. I'm also in some initial discussions concerning the possible purchase of another hospital. Any scandal at one of our facilities would have a devastating effect on our stock price and most likely scuttle any acquisition efforts. If illegal activities are, in fact, going on at Mercy, I need to have irrefutable evidence before I bring in any law enforcement agency.

"I'd like you to use your computer expertise to penetrate Mercy's security system and look for irregularities in narcotics ordering, delivery, and usage. In other words, find out what the hell's going on!"

"That shouldn't present a major problem."

"Good. You'll need a cover story should anyone discover your activities. That's where your cybersecurity reputation comes into play. If you're willing to do this, I'll direct Vice President Summerton to hire your firm to analyze and report on the security of our patient information. This will give you the necessary cover to enter our computer systems and, hopefully, find the source of the irregularities and possible theft of narcotics. If you decide to accept my offer, you need to understand that you'll be out there on your own."

Allen smiled. "My regular fee for a complete cybersecurity analysis is $25,000. If that works for you, you got yourself your computer mole, and you can rest assured our arrangement will remain secure."

"I never doubted your ability to keep a secret, Allen." Rennells reached into his briefcase and removed a burner phone. "Use this to contact me in case of emergency. I'll give you my private number. Unless an emergency does occur, you are not to contact me or Mr. Summerton until you've uncovered the source of the problem. Like I said, I'll need names and hard evidence before I go to the authorities. Understood?"

"Yes, sir."

Jack and Allen shook hands. On the way out of the library, Jack told Allen he would be receiving a phone call from Summerton early the following week requesting a meeting at Mercy General.

Back in the living room, Jack shook Julius' hand, kissed Elizabeth on the cheek, and thanked them both for their hospitality. Julius, Elizabeth, and Allen walked Rennells outside to his waiting limo.

"Thanks for stopping by," Julius said. "And don't be a stranger. You know you're always welcome here in Charleston."

"I know, Jack, and the same goes for you and Elizabeth in Chicago." Jack looked at Allen, gave a quick nod, then slid into the backseat of the limousine.

CHAPTER EIGHT

IT WAS CLOSE to 4:00 in the afternoon when Nick and Josh finished a "Shack" session with Bullet, one of their newer dogs. They'd built a simple 20' X 20' wooden building with two rooms and a variety of shelves, cabinets, and sealed compartments. They called the building the "Shack" and used it to train for narcotics and explosives detection.

Detection dogs, commonly referred to as "sniffers," use their unique sense of smell to locate specific objects based on the scent of the object. For example, handlers train their sniffers to associate the smell of drugs with their favorite toy. In reality, the dog could care less about the drugs themselves. Most often a rolled up white towel is used at the toy. Dogs love to play a game of tug-of-war with their favorite towel. The handler simply plays with the dog and the towel, which has been carefully washed so that it has no scent of its own. Later, a drug like marijuana is rolled up inside the towel, and after playing for a while, the dog starts to recognize the smell of marijuana as the smell of his favorite toy. The handler then hides the towel, with the drugs, in various places. As training progresses, different drugs are placed in the towel, until the dog is able to sniff out a variety of illegal substances. The same method is used for bomb-detection dogs, except various chemicals used to manufacture explosives are placed in the towel instead of drugs.

After they'd spent twenty minutes inside the hundred-plus degree building, Nick turned to Josh and said, "Okay, that's it for today."

Outside, Nick filled Bullet's water dish and tossed a plastic water bottle to Josh, who immediately poured half over his head. "Christ, it's hot!" he muttered. "Feels like I'm back in Afghanistan!"

"Those days are over, my friend," Nick said. "Let's get this dog cooled down, and I believe there just might be some cold drinks waiting for us in the office."

"Roger that!" Josh gasped, as he led Bullet back to the kennels. "I'll get the dogs settled down and lock up. See you back in the office."

"Thanks. Go ahead and leave the kennel fans on low. We'll let them run all night. And check to make sure Isaiah left them enough water."

About fifteen minutes later, Josh walked into the air-conditioned trailer, went directly to the makeshift kitchen, and grabbed himself a Holy City IPA.

Nick was already working on his second Coke, and Sally was nursing her ice tea. Once Josh was settled, Nick said, "Okay, folks, listen up. I had an interesting phone call last week from Lieutenant Steve Williams, my old boss with the K-9 Unit. Before Steve joined the force, he was a Sargent stationed at Lackland Air Force base in Texas." Nick smiled at Josh, who had suddenly become noticeably attentive. Lackland housed one of the government's largest K-9 training facilities, putting out over six hundred dogs a year as the TSA's primary supplier. Nick continued, "And I think you know what goes on at Lackland. Right, Josh?"

"Holy shit, Nick! Oops. Sorry about that, Sally. But that's one of the largest K-9 training facilities the government has. That training center puts out a ton of dogs a year. Just about all TSA dogs are trained at Lackland. What'd he say?"

"Well, apparently, with the elevated terrorist threats, Lackland can't quite keep up with the demand for TSA dogs. Steve has a good buddy at Lackland who asked him if he knew anyone that could help supply some dogs until the DOD can ramp up their training capabilities."

By this time Josh was out of his seat. "Tell me we got an order!"

Nick nodded. "I just received a verbal order confirmation for six explosive sniffers with additional orders in the pipeline if we can deliver the first six dogs in eight weeks. I checked with one of our breeders in Georgia, and he promised me he's got plenty of green one-year old dogs that are 100% ready for training."

Josh's enthusiasm quickly dimmed. "Nick, that's great news, but we've already got twelve dogs in different stages of training right now and a backlog of orders. How are we gonna make this thing happen?"

"That's where the VA comes in," Nick said. "I checked with the counselor that hooked us up, and he knows an ex-Army K-9 handler out in Savannah, a guy named Zachary Brown, that could use some help just like you did. I'd like you to drive down there tomorrow and, if you think he's got what it takes, sign him up and get him back here pronto! If you think he's not ready, don't do it.

We can't afford to mess this one up. Sally, you can look into finding this guy a temporary place to stay and get the paperwork ready."

Josh shook Nick's hand and with a sly smile said, "I guess I can forget about that fishing vacation."

Nick laughed. "I think we're all in the same boat for a while!"

Sally had some paperwork to finish up and told Nick she'd make sure the motion sensors were turned on and the security gate was locked before she left.

Nick missed the traffic window to downtown, and his normal twenty-five-minute commute turned into an hour of stop-and-go as cars crawled across both the Johns and James Island connectors and trickled from Route 30 onto Lockwood Drive. It was a shade after 6:00 by the time he finally made it back to his condo's garage.

Nick was thinking through all the things that needed to get done as he stepped into the garage elevator. Just as the door was about to close, a fellow carrying a small lamp and two large Walmart bags squeezed inside. Noticing the guy had both hands occupied with what he was carrying, Nick asked, "What floor?"

"Six, please. Thanks, appreciate that."

Nick's condo was also on the sixth floor, but he didn't recognize the man. "Mine, too. You just moving in?"

"Yeah," he said, lifting the bags and lamp. "Still trying to make the place livable."

"I know what you mean. I've been here for years, and I'm still working on it. Good to meet you. I'm Nick. In 612."

"Thanks, Nick. Right down the hall from you in 624. I'm Allen Miller. Nice to meet you."

"Welcome home, Allen."

CHAPTER NINE

NICK WAS WAITING in line at The Coffee Cup, and once he got to the counter he smiled at Amy and started their regular morning ritual, "Good morning, Amy. How's school treating you?"

"Keepin' me busy, Nick. That's for sure!" Amy already had his coffee poured and his blueberry muffin bagged by the time he made it to the counter at The Cup. At least, he assumed it was a blueberry muffin. Last week she had playfully sabotaged his usual morning ritual by slipping him a sesame bagel. He was halfway through it before he looked up and caught her smirking at him. He pointedly checked the bag before leaving her a ten-dollar bill and joining Angela, who was waving him over to her usual table.

"Hey! How many lives do you expect to save today?"

"Probably more than usual. This heat has made folks stupid. How are the dogs taking it?"

"They don't complain half as much as their trainers. What's up with you this weekend?"

Angela rolled her eyes and said, "Got a hot date tonight. Taking my mom to a potluck dinner at her church. Can't wait!"

"You're a good girl, Angela. Keep that karma thing working for you." Nick was listening to Angela describe what it was like to spend three hours in a church basement eating meatloaf and talking about Jesus when he noticed the guy he met the night before on the elevator. "Angela, I'll be right back. Got someone I want you to meet."

Allen Miller was just leaving the counter when Nick caught him. "Allen, 624, right?" Nick pointed toward Angela and said, "I'm at that table over there. Wanna join us?"

Allen was caught off guard, but managed to say, "Nick, 612, right? Sure. Lead the way."

Nick introduced him to Angela and explained that Allen had just moved onto the same floor in his building. "Angela's an emergency room nurse over at Mercy General Hospital. She's a regular angel of mercy."

"I don't know about that, Nick," Angela said. "Allen, nice to meet you." After exchanging pleasantries, Angela asked Allen about his work.

Allen paused before answering. "I've got a small computer firm over on Queen Street. Actually, it's just me and an assistant. I do some work with computer systems and write some software. Nothing too exciting." Allen then turned to Nick and said, "Your turn. What gets you up in the morning?"

"I have a small company out on Johns Island. We train police dogs. Get to work with man's best friend every day. Can't complain about that." Nick looked at his watch and said, "Sorry guys, gotta run. Allen, see you around the building. Oh, and Angela, have a blast tonight at that wild party!" Nick left her trying to explain what this "wild party" was really all about.

Allen and Angela hit it off. When they left for work, he walked her to the hospital and then continued on to his office. Even after living in downtown Charleston for most of his life, Allen never tired of the city…its history, its nightlife, but most of all, its people with their genuine congeniality that seemed to be ingrained in the spirit of the city.

Allen's office was, to say the least, a bit unusual when it came to its décor. The two windows on the far wall were covered with opaque, sun-canceling black paint. Recessed lighting emitted a soft glow, much like you might find in a nightclub. Two Scandinavian white leather chairs sat in front of a simple but obviously expensive smoked glass executive desk, which faced the door. The high back swivel chair behind the desk was the same white leather.

But the most extraordinary aspect of the office was the five-screen array of ASUS ProArt 46" computer monitors and three IKEY DT stainless steel keyboards; each interfaced with CoreMC-2 computer towers using high-speed XREON 6 processors. The space behind the computer systems looked like a spaghetti factory. This was Allen's comfort zone, the place he could explore the nooks and crannies of the web, stealthily entering those seemingly invisible holes and portals that existed in virtually every computer system.

There were several free-standing white boards used to list critical data and construct flow charts to create a visual landscape of his projects. An eclectic combination of black and white posters hung on the walls, including pictures of Christopher Columbus, James Bond, Sherlock Holmes, and David Bowie.

Sarah grabbed her notebook and pen and followed Allen into his office. She still couldn't get over how strange Allen's office was, with all the computer equipment, weird lighting, and posters. The first time she saw it, she told him it reminded her of Star Trek's USS Enterprise, and she expected Captain Kirk and Spock to be beamed up any second. She gave Allen a plastic model of the Enterprise and a plaque for his birthday. The model sat on his desk, and the plaque, which he proudly displayed on his office door, read:

CyberSpace: The Final Frontier.
These are the voyages of the starship CyberNet. Its
continuing mission: to explore strange new worlds,
to seek out new networks, and discover new
cybersystems...
...to boldly go where no one has gone before!

Sarah got cozy in one of the white leather chairs and said, "What's up?"

"We just got a new client. I had a meeting yesterday regarding some irregularities at Mercy General Hospital here in Charleston." Allen went on to explain what went on in his meeting with MediGroup's CEO, Jack Rennells, and the strange situation at Mercy. "We'll need to put aside what we're working on now and concentrate on getting to the bottom of what's going on at Mercy. First of all, I need you to get me everything you can find on MediGroup financials. It's headquartered in Chicago and basically acts as a holding company for several hospitals and other medical facilities located primarily in the Midwest and South. Also, see what you can put together on Mercy: number of beds, ICUs, different surgical units, etc. I'll start researching PharmaTech and look into some of the key players, like Rennells, Summerton, Fitzgerald, etc. I'll also familiarize myself with the typical supply chain of drugs from the time they leave the manufacturer until they're delivered to hospitals and administered to the patients."

"Got it," Sarah said.

Allen and Sarah spent most of the day hunkered down in the office gathering basic information Allen would need before he attempted to access Mercy General's internal network. The more he knew about a company or individual prior to the actual hack, the more productive the hack was. Allen had started to look into the typical process involved in the ordering, receiving, and distributing of narcotics within the hospital environment, when he remembered that Angela worked at Mercy. He'd only known her for a short time, but they'd seem to connect. She'd definitely be a wealth of information when it came to hospital personnel, but he'd have to weigh the risk. The fewer people involved the better the chances his search would stay covert. He set the thought aside for the time being.

Allen continued to work until he called it a day and left the office a little past 7:00. But once he got back to his condo, he couldn't help himself and dove back in. He brewed a pot of coffee and sat down at the kitchen table with his work. During his time in Washington, he'd developed an appreciation of jazz and frequented clubs there like the Blues Alley, the Bohemian Caverns, Chaz Billy's, and many of the other nightclubs and restaurants featuring music from some of the greats. He opened Spotify and queued up his jazz playlist, which included hits from Charles Mingus, John Coltrane, Herbie Hancock, and Thelonious Monk.

He spent another hour or so listening to jazz and reviewing the info he'd compiled that day. The work was an all-day affair, and Allen knew there would be many more to come before this job was done.

CHAPTER TEN

IT WAS SATURDAY evening, and Nick had just taken a leisurely twenty-minute stroll to AC's on King Street. He took a seat at the bar and ordered a Holy City IPA. He'd sworn off the hard stuff after his battle with the bottle the year after the shooting and limited himself to no more than two or three beers a night. He'd never forget the hell he'd been through and wasn't about to give up the life he'd fought so hard to rebuild. He felt his cellphone vibrate in his pocket. It was Josh. "Josh, what's shakin?"

"Hey, Nick. Driving back from Savannah. Spent most of the afternoon with your boy, Zach Brown."

"Great. What'd you think?"

"He's a keeper. Seemed to have all the necessary K-9 handling skills. He's had multiple tours in Afghanistan, so he's got some baggage, but I think we should give him a chance. Remember where my head was when you brought me on. Anyway, you told me to hire him if I thought he'd work out, so I did. He's driving up here on Tuesday."

"Sounds good. At least he has the war behind him," said Nick.

"The war may be behind him, Nick, but for any soldier, coming home is always a battle."

"I hear you, Josh. I need to check with Sally. She was going to look into some places he could stay if he worked out."

"No need to do that. I have a second bedroom at my place. I told Zach he could bunk with me for awhile. I also want to make sure he can handle the change. He's still a little shaky from his disability discharge, but he's Army, and we take care of our own."

"I trust your judgment. Let's plan on meeting tomorrow about noon at the James Island Lowe's. We need to get to work on those new kennels for the six new dogs coming in from Georgia."

"Sounds like a plan. See you tomorrow, Nick. Have a good night."

"Drive carefully," said Nick as he disconnected the call and slid his phone back into his pocket.

Nick got his beer, ordered a sandwich, and started to think about all he'd been through the last ten years: the time on the force, a year recovery with his dad, the last five hectic years building his business. He'd dated off and on, and even had a few semi-serious relationships, but none of them lasted.

Living by himself, Nick would often grab a bite to eat at AC's or one of the other downtown spots within walking distance. He glanced around the bar which reminded himself how he'd never really got into the whole bar scene, with the exception of his late-night forays into some of the more seedy bars during his battle with drinking after the shooting. Now in his mid-thirties, Nick often thought it would be nice to meet someone and settle down, but the demands of starting and running his company put a major damper on his social life. Maybe he should give it a try with Amy. They had fun the few times they'd been out together, but those weren't dates. They were always with groups of friends. But they were definitely comfortable with each other, and he was pretty sure she wasn't involved with someone else.

Nick finished his meal, paid the check, and left AC's. Walking back to his condo, he couldn't get Amy out of his mind. He had a successful company, some good friends, and a nice place to live, but there was definitely something missing in his life. Maybe Amy was that missing piece. There was only one way to find out, and Nick was ready to make that happen.

CHAPTER ELEVEN

ALLEN WAS UP bright and early Sunday morning, and after a six-mile run around the streets of Charleston, he showered and ate a bowl of cereal and some fruit for breakfast. He threw on a pair of shorts and one of his old MIT sweatshirts and headed to his office to put in a few more hours of research.

He spent the rest of the morning compiling more information about narcotics and how pharmacies and hospitals use and distribute these drugs. Allen knew the opioid addiction was a serious problem in the U.S., but he was amazed at the extent the epidemic had grown in recent years. Almost 64,000 people died of overdoses in 2016, well beyond the total number of U.S. deaths in the entire Vietnam War. With only 5% of the world's population, the U.S. consumes 99% of the powerful pain killer hydrocodone and over 80% of the world's supply of opioids. Over 750,000 prescriptions for these controlled substances are filled each day in the United States—over fifteen million pills every day not counting those administered in hospitals!

It was no surprise organized crime has become a major player in the opioid trade. The cost of one oxycodone or Oxycontin pill, purchased legally by a pharmacy or hospital, is about seventeen cents, but that same pill could bring between ten and thirty dollars on the street. Dilaudid, fentanyl, and other pain-related narcotics demand similar street values.

Despite state and federal programs to control the problem, the illegal flow of these prescription drugs continues to increase at an alarming rate. Private treatment centers can run between $20,000 to $50,000 a month, well beyond the reach of typical addicts. And the wait to get into government sponsored detox programs can be weeks or even months, which is like waiting a week for a life raft on the Titanic.

Much of the effort to deal with narcotic theft has been focused on controlling the drugs in the pharmacies and hospitals, but recent studies indicated that the majority of drugs are stolen in-transit or at the point of delivery to pharmacies and hospitals. The more Allen dug into the subject, the more he believed that if there was serious narcotic theft going on at Mercy—and the profit margins certainly indicated that there was—it was likely happening when the drugs arrived at the hospital.

Allen believed there was a good chance that the deteriorating health of Chris Davis, Chuck Thompson's recent abrupt departure, and the unexpected turnover in the shipping department were all linked to the problem. PharmaTec's appearance on the scene was another suspicious piece of the puzzle. These theories could be verified or disproved once Allen was able to hack into Mercy's system and gain access to their internal documents and communications. Then he could track the drugs from initial orders to the final distribution to patients. Once Allen was familiar with the flow of drugs through Mercy, he'd be able to figure out if and how the process was compromised.

After another hour or so of research, Allen left his office and spent the rest of the afternoon picking up odds and ends for his new home. Back at his condo, he enjoyed a quiet evening. Evenings like this would be few and far between until the MediGroup assignment was completed.

CHAPTER TWELVE

NICK WAS UP early Sunday morning and got ahold of Josh Taylor to confirm they'd meet at noon at the local James Island Lowe's store to load the materials needed to build the new kennels.

It was close to 1:30 by the time Nick and Josh arrived at the Academy. Josh was quite the handyman and had brought all the tools necessary to get the job done. By 6:00, they had the framing and walls completed and roof installed. They were both bushed and agreed to finish installing the wire mesh and doors in the morning and headed to the office for a beer or two.

"So," Nick said, "tell me more about this Zach Brown. Didn't really get a chance to discuss it with you last night."

"Big black guy," said Josh. "Must go about six five and two fifty. He looks like a strip club bouncer, but he's very soft spoken, which doesn't surprise me, based on what he went through over in Afghanistan. Spent a few hours with him and was fairly impressed with his knowledge of training and handling. He was stationed at Fort Benning in Georgia, where I got my training. I called my old

CO at Benning, and he told me Zach was a solid soldier. To tell you the truth, Nick, I think he's probably in better mental shape than I was when you saved my ass."

"Okay," Nick said, "the six dogs we'll be getting on Wednesday are to be trained in explosives detection. That's your expertise, so you can get Zach started. I'd like him to work with the new dogs, but I'm going to rely on you to monitor him, and tell me if he can't cut it. We've got eight weeks to deliver those dogs to the TSA, and we can't mess this up."

"Don't worry, Nick. I'll keep an eye on him."

Nick and Josh spent another half an hour talking about the new dogs that would be delivered Wednesday, and how to start their training. It was approaching 7:00 by the time they left the Academy and headed home.

CHAPTER THIRTEEN

AFTER GRABBING HIS usual coffee and muffin at The Cup on Monday morning, Nick headed out to Johns Island to finish the temporary kennels. Josh was already working when Nick arrived twenty-five minutes later. It was after noon by the time they installed the doors and finished mixing and pouring the concrete. The finished product left much to be desired compared to the original twelve kennels, but they would get the job done.

~~~~

The next day, the crew was in the office eating lunch when an older model Ford-150 turned into the lot and parked next to the trailer. Sally looked out the window and simply said, "Oh my," when she saw the man get out of the truck and begin to survey the grounds. Josh joined Sally at the window then opened the trailer door and waved Zach over.

Josh was not kidding when he said Zach was an enormous dude. His head was clean-shaven, and he wore army boots, black
~~~~

jeans, and a black T-shirt that was stretched tight across a huge chest and shoulders the size of bowling balls. His arms could be easily mistaken for tree trunks. Zach nodded at Josh and slowly sauntered to the trailer, taking in his new surroundings as he went.

He ducked as he entered, and Josh introduced him to everyone. He nodded and shook Nick's hand but said nothing. Josh nodded toward Sally. "Zach, say hello to Sally Reed. She's the real boss around here."

Zach nodded again and simply said, "Ma'am." When he was finally introduced to Isaiah, Zach stood up a bit straighter and said, "Afternoon, sir."

Isaiah shook his hand and said, "Afternoon, son. Welcome to the Academy."

There was a short awkward silence until Nick added, "Zach, it's good to have you. Josh's spoken highly of you, and we all want you to feel at home here. Can I get you something to drink? We've got Coke or iced tea."

"Iced tea would be nice, sir."

"Iced tea, it is," Nick said. "And please, Zach, call me Nick. We're informal around here."

"Yes, sir."

"Have a seat, Zach," Josh said with a smile. "How was the drive up from Savannah?"

"Fine, sir," Zach said and took a seat in a plastic chair—one that, Nick feared, wouldn't have the stamina or inclination to support Zach.

Nick poured an iced tea for Zach, who nodded a polite thank you. Isaiah took the floor and began a lengthy dissertation on the history of Johns Island until Josh finally interrupted and said, "Zach, why don't Nick and I give you a quick tour of the grounds.

I know Sally has some paperwork she needs you to fill out when we're done."

Josh and Nick spent the next forty-five minutes walking Zach around the facility answering the few questions he had. Zach seemed eager to spend time with the dogs, so Josh brought out Bullet and ran him through some basic hand signals. Before long, Zach was handling Bullet by himself. Josh caught Nick's eye and smiled. Nick returned the smile and gave him a thumbs up.

CHAPTER FOURTEEN

THE MORE INFORMATION you can acquire regarding a person or entity prior to initiating the hack is a critical element to its success, and the internet is full of it. Most people forget that the convenient access provided by the digital world is a two-way street. Just the basic tools of an internet search can reel in a stranger's account number and the street their mother lived on in the second grade. Even with an arsenal of sophisticated software at his disposal, Allen knew there was no substitute for the kind of advance intelligence gathered by patient research. Like many other kinds of covert operations, the most successful hacks are built on the backs of a thoroughly compiled database. In addition to digital information, the development of "live intel," or information obtained from individuals who know the target person or entity, can generate real time information that will also help to focus the hack.

Allen and Sarah continued their background research for the next few days and filled the office's whiteboards with flow charts and information they'd gathered on the companies involved and their key personnel.

It was about 1:00 Wednesday afternoon when Allen and Sarah first met in his office to begin reviewing and analyzing their research. Once Sarah was situated, Nick said, "Sarah, go ahead and give me a recap of what you've found."

For the next hour, Sarah presented what she'd compiled on both MediGroup and Mercy General. "Okay, MediGroup was created in 1980 by a venture capital company that purchased three hospitals in Indiana. Over the next thirty-five years, the company grew through the acquisition of twenty-five more hospitals in several Midwest and Southern states. They also acquired four nursing homes, and lately have picked up several private urgent care facilities. The hospitals are all small to medium-sized and located in or around major cities. Mercy General was acquired three years ago along with two other hospitals—one in Columbia, South Carolina and another in Savannah, Georgia. The hospital segment of the business generates well over ninety percent of their income.

"MediGroup's stock went public in 2005, when it was listed on the NASDAQ, and has historically performed well when compared to other companies in the medical market segment. Mr. Rennells was made CEO of MediGroup shortly after it went public, and he has an excellent reputation. He's also very active in representing the industry in Washington DC. Mercy General enjoys an excellent reputation and has been a profitable medium-sized hospital with approximately two hundred seventy-five beds."

Sarah finished her presentation by reviewing the whiteboard diagram she had created showing the structure of both MediGroup and Mercy General along with an analysis of the available financial information for both.

"Nice job, Sarah." Allen then began to explain his findings regarding the typical ordering process, major manufacturers, and channels of distribution for prescription pharmaceuticals in the United States. He had made a fairly intricate flowchart on one of the whiteboards showing the movement of drugs from manufacturer to patient. Both federal and state government agencies, as well as independent pharmacies and hospitals, had instituted strict regulations surrounding the distribution of these controlled substances. Like in most areas of the hospital, digital files had replaced much of the traditional paperwork in the purchasing process for narcotics and other pharmaceutical products making their ordering relatively straightforward.

Narcotics, like other medicines, were rarely purchased from the manufacturer but rather supplied through regional distributors and local warehousing centers. Pharmacists would submit a list of drugs required to the hospital purchasing department. The purchasing department would then consolidate the order, prepare the paperwork, and issue an electronic purchase order to the appropriate distribution center. Regular pharmacy orders were submitted on a weekly basis and typically delivered to Mercy on Fridays with special orders processed and delivered when necessary. Delivery of a specific drug order was typically made by the local distributor's truck or by Federal Express deliveries when smaller or special orders were required.

All narcotics and specialized drugs were delivered in sealed containers to be opened and itemized by the hospital's shipping and receiving department. Mercy General had recently instituted detailed employee background checks for all shipping and receiving personnel. These background checks were initiated by the personnel department and executed by Mercy General's internal security staff.

The cybersecurity department was responsible for the monitoring and review of a comprehensive system of digital security cameras that had been installed throughout the facility. Pharmacists could only receive their drug order after it had been accepted by shipping department personnel and checked against the specific purchasing order. In addition, several unannounced spot checks of shipping employees were made periodically as another safeguard against drug theft.

"Studies show that while the incidents of narcotic theft by nurses, doctors, and pharmacists are on the rise," Allen said, "they still constitute a much smaller percentage of overall loss when compared to the amounts of drugs lost in transit. I doubt that any change in the theft of drugs by hospital personnel would be enough to cause the pharmacy's recent accounting problems. I will be able to verify this when I access the hospital's computer systems and view their internal documents."

"So, it sounds like the major potential for theft is probably when the drugs are delivered to Mercy's shipping department," Sarah said.

"Exactly," Allen said. "But, assuming the delivery of the narcotics matches the purchasing paperwork, why does the pharmacy now have to order more drugs than usual? It's clear something has changed, so let's focus on the recent changes we know about: PharmaTech took over the pharmacy, there were changes in the Purchasing Department, and there were changes in the shipping and receiving department."

"Right," Sarah said, "we know PharmaTech was brought in to reduce costs, and that's obviously not working. So, it's got to be in the pharmacy or somewhere in purchasing or shipping."

"Okay, now let's look at the key personnel at Mercy." Allen had researched the business and personal histories of Charles Summerton, Blake Fitzgerald, Russ Slean, Chris Davis, Chuck Thompson, and a few other key players. He made lists for each person, identifying things like hometown, schools attended, previous employment, associations, clubs, etc.—looking for points in their past where one or more of them may have intersected. Allen and Sarah spent some time reviewing and crosschecking the lists but, with the exception of memberships in some industry associations, neither could find anything linking them prior to working at Mercy General. The exercise seemed to be a dead end.

It was approaching 6:00, when Allen said, "All right, let's call it quits for today. I'll get inside Mercy's computer system tomorrow and see what I can find. I also met a nurse who works at Mercy, so she may be a good source of information once I get a better understanding of drug flow in the hospital and key players we're dealing with. Plus, I need to pick up few more things for the condo."

"Well, at least you have your priorities straight!" Sarah said with a laugh. "Have a good night, and I'll see you in the morning."

CHAPTER FIFTEEN

ALLEN WAS UP early Thursday morning and in his office shortly after 7:00.

The ultimate goal of accessing a company's computer network and its internal data is to achieve remote "Root Access." Once a hacker obtains this level of access, he basically has complete control over a particular computer system and all its information. There are a variety of tools available to achieve this level of control, such as keylogging, system scan, phishing, Dirty COW (copy-on-write), packet sniffers, etc. It took Allen less than an hour to bypass system firewalls and gain complete control over Mercy's computer systems. Thousands of successful hacks over the years had not diminished the euphoric thrill he felt with each new event. Allen was on the hunt. Someone asked him once what it felt like to achieve Root Access. He said it sounded a little creepy, but it was like secretly entering someone's house and watching the members of its family go about their private lives completely unaware of his presence.

Allen was not a believer in coincidence, never had been. Where some people saw coincidence, he saw conspiracy. That was his job. Mercy's accountant, Russ Slean, had ruled out simple accounting error. Drugs at Mercy were not just disappearing into thin air. It was clear to Allen—someone was stealing them.

A simple search of the personnel department's emails uncovered several memorandums dealing with PharmaTech and the disposition of Chris Davis and Chuck Thompson. One inter-office memo announced that PharmaTech's Mr. Ken Tanaka would act as the new Chief Pharmacy Officer for Mercy General.

Allen first wanted to familiarize himself with both Davis and Thompson. He needed to learn what caused Davis's illness and Thompson's sudden resignation from the hospital. Both had been exemplary employees who worked their way up to key positions within the hospital.

Davis was forty and had no substantive health problems prior to his recent illness. He was an avid runner and religiously worked out in the hospital's fitness center. Entries in his personnel file, along with specific emails related to his illness, indicated that he seemed depressed and had experienced a heightened heart rate, fatigue, chest pain, and swelling in his legs and ankles. All these symptoms pointed to kidney failure. Because he was treated at Mercy, Allen was able to access his medical records, which showed a surprising result from his kidney biopsy. The biopsy disclosed the presence of oxalate crystals, a clear indication that he had been exposed to ethylene glycol, the key ingredient in antifreeze and deicing agents. Ethylene glycol is a colorless and tasteless liquid, and as crazy as it sounded, somehow Chris Davis must have ingested it in some form or another. Swallowing ethylene glycol was a fairly common method used by individuals attempting suicide, but there was absolutely no evidence that Chris Davis was a candidate to take his own life. Since any accidental ingestion was incredibly unlikely, foul play seemed like a definite possibility. Despite multiple attempts, Allen could not discover evidence of how the ethylene glycol might have been administered or who may have been involved. Another dead end.

The personnel department had issued an internal announcement addressing Mr. Davis's decision to take a temporary leave of absence due to health considerations, and that his assistant, Kate Parker, would be assuming his duties until such time that Mr. Davis could return to his position.

Allen now turned his attention to Chuck Thompson. His decision to leave Mercy General seemed to have come out of the blue. Brad Strickland, an assistant in the shipping department, was made acting department manager until a formal replacement could be hired. Like Davis, Thompson was in excellent health and was extremely competent in his position as the manager of the shipping department. Allen spent a fair amount of time reviewing Thompson's personnel file and scanning his emails during the period right before his resignation. The search uncovered nothing that might have explained his sudden departure, but Allen was convinced it was related to Chris Davis's illness and the high rate of turnover in his department. If there was a connection, Allen had no doubt he would eventually find it.

Allen's foray into Mercy's personnel files had uncovered three new persons of interest: Ken Tanaka, PharmaTech's Chief Pharmacy Officer; Kate Parker in purchasing; and Brad Strickland in shipping and receiving. Like he had done with other key personnel, Allen used hospital files to thoroughly research the three new targets looking for points in their past where one or more of them may have intersected with other key players. Again, the exercise seemed to be fruitless, so he called Sarah into his office to see if she might catch a connection that he was missing.

"Look, Allen," Sarah finally said, "I have to admit that, at first, I was convinced that PharmaTech had to be behind the problem. The whole thing with the reduction in profit margin occurred shortly after the company was brought on. But, the more I thought about it, the more it didn't make sense. Once PharmaTech was brought on, you'd expect margins to improve, not the opposite!"

Allen smiled and said, "Well, maybe they're just a terribly inefficient operation."

Sarah shook her head. "I don't buy that and neither do you. I checked them out, and they've got a good track record with their other clients. I think it's got to be somewhere in purchasing or shipping. The situations with Davis and Thompson are definitely related and have got to be somehow connected to the disappearance of narcotics."

"You're probably right," Allen said, "but we still don't have any hard evidence that would explain their involvement. While both departments might be culpable, I tend to think the shipping department is the key player—that is, if the drugs are in fact being stolen, which I have little doubt that they are. They're the folks that actually handle the shipments and check them against the orders produced by purchasing. I've accessed the five shipping department security cameras and downloaded the footage. They need to be reviewed to see if anything looks suspicious. These cameras are motion-activated and carry date and time notations. I've downloaded the last three weeks, so there's quite a bit of footage to review. I'll continue to see what information I can find on some of the other key people at Mercy General."

Sarah smiled. "It looks like I'm going to the movies. Send me the files, and I'll get on it."

CHAPTER SIXTEEN

IT WAS FRIDAY morning at The Cup. Nick grabbed his muffin and coffee then joined Angela and Allen at a corner table. "Hi, Nick. TGIF!" said Angela. "Got anything exciting going on this weekend?"

"Well, now that you mention it, I do. I'm having a little get together Sunday afternoon out at the Academy. We're celebrating a nice order from the TSA and welcoming a new trainer. I was hoping you guys could join us. Nothing fancy, just some beer, wine, hot dogs, and burgers."

"Sounds fun," Angela said. "I'm taking my mom to church Sunday morning, and I don't know if you've ever been to a black service, but they can go on all day. A day out at your place sounds a lot more exciting, and this'll give me a good excuse to gracefully bow out early."

"Sounds good," said Allen. "I could use some fun and excitement in my life right now."

Nick laughed. "Well, I'm not too sure there'll be a lot of excitement, but it should be fun, and we're supposed to get a break from the heat this weekend." Nick gave Angela and Allen his telephone number and the address of the Academy before they headed off to work. He was happy they were coming, but the reason he gave for the party wasn't accurate—it was really an excuse to see if he could get together with Amy.

He finished his coffee and muffin and waited until there was no line before approaching Amy. Nick had to laugh, here he was, in his mid-thirties, feeling like he was about to ask a cheerleader to the prom. He took a deep breath. "Hi, Amy. You know, well, I was thinking, I'm having some people out to my kennels this Sunday. Angela and Allen are coming, and I wondered if you were free and might like to come with me."

Amy smiled and her luminous green eyes seemed to twinkle.

Nick returned her smile and sheepishly said, "I'm sorry, Amy. If you're busy, we can—"

"Don't be silly," she interrupted. "I'd love to. This'll be a first for me. I've never been asked out on a date to go to a dog kennel before. What time on Sunday?"

"I can pick you up around two, if that works for you?"

"That's perfect. I'm opening on Sunday, but I'll be done just before then."

"Works for me. See you on Sunday."

Nick turned to leave but stopped and turned back with a big smile on his face. "Oh, and by the way, you look really nice, Amy." That smile stayed on his face all the way out to Johns Island.

CHAPTER SEVENTEEN

BY THE TIME Allen got into the office on Friday morning, Sarah had already spent a few hours reviewing security footage from the hospital's shipping department. "Golly, Boss," she said sarcastically when he came in, "I had no idea how exciting this cyber stuff was going to be. I'm really getting into watching these guys unload boxes."

"Glad you're enthralled. Have you noticed anything out of the ordinary yet?"

"Nope."

"Well, hang in there. If something fishy's going on, chances are it's on those files."

Once settled in his office, Allen proceeded with the assumption that Davis' illness and Thompson's resignation were related and had something to do with the narcotics problem at Mercy.

He repeated the previous day's procedure and was now able to access Mercy's network in a matter of thirty minutes. He began by combing through Chuck Thompson's phone records starting three weeks prior to his abrupt resignation as the manager of the shipping department. Most calls made to the hospital came into the main switchboard receptionist, but Thompson, like other department heads, had his own direct line. Once Allen identified the phone records, he downloaded the individual numbers and applied a program to sort each number based on call frequency during that time period. By doing this, he was able to separate the numbers that were most likely made or received in the normal course of business with those that appeared only a few times. The assumption being that the higher the frequency, the more likely the call was related to business, and the lower the frequency the more likely it was not. The obvious exceptions were the numbers belonging to his home phone and his wife's cell. The sort came up with eleven numbers that appeared three or fewer times over that three-week span.

Allen had accessed Thompson's personnel file the day before and noted that his unexpected resignation had occurred the afternoon of Thursday, July 13th at approximately 3:00. It was also noted that he was interviewed at that time and, after collecting some personal items, immediately left the hospital, refusing to give the normal two-week notice. Allen then listed those eleven phone calls in chronological order leading up to the day and time of his resignation. Of the eleven numbers, only one came in on the day Thompson resigned. The number was an incoming call from (843) 555-3763, a local Charleston number.

Allen then used one of the many reverse phone directories available on the internet to identify the name and address of the individual or company from which the call was made. The number was no longer "In Network," and Allen had no luck finding additional information. He assumed this meant the call came from a burner phone that had since been destroyed. It was a long shot, and Allen wasn't convinced it would lead anywhere, but it was a simple exercise and might be worth the effort. He got up, walked to one of the whiteboards, and wrote down the number, adding a question mark in a bright red marker.

Chuck Thompson's personnel file showed that his bi-monthly salary check had been direct-deposited into a local bank. After Allen identified Thompson's personal email address from company records, it was easy to get his password. Thompson made a common mistake—using the same password for almost everything. Sure enough, the password for Thompson's bank matched the one he used for his email accounts, thus allowing Allen easy access to his banking records. Both his checking and savings account showed minimal balances, and it didn't take long to discover that there had been a series of $7,500 monthly withdrawals made from his savings account over a period of ten months ending in July of this year. While there may have been perfectly valid reasons for the withdrawals, they were definitely suspect—the funds in his savings account ran out in July, the same month he unexpectedly resigned from Mercy General.

Allen was beginning to feel a tinge of excitement. He next searched Thompson's web history using the same program to sort sites visited by frequency. The most frequented sites were those you would expect: his bank, weather, CNN, FOX Sports. But *bovada.lv.com* had been visited on an almost daily basis. When Allen searched the site, pieces of the puzzle began to fall into place— Bovada was an online betting site! Allen smiled and thought, *Well, well, looks like our friend, Chuck, just might have himself a bit of a gambling problem.*

CHAPTER EIGHTEEN

THE FORECASTED COLD front did arrive late Saturday afternoon, and Sunday's highs were expected to be in the mid-70s. An unusual dip in the jet stream brought about the welcomed lower temperatures and humidity to many Southern states and a premature glimpse of autumn in Charleston.

Nick was out at the Academy early Sunday morning straightening up the office and policing the grounds. He'd picked up a small keg of beer from Johns Island's Low Tide Brewing on Saturday afternoon and set it up outside the office under one of the several live oaks that graced his property. One of the many perks of living and working on Johns Island was the abundance of old live oak trees with Spanish moss hanging from their huge wooden tentacles like long gray beards. Johns Island is the home of the famous Angel Oak, thought to be the oldest tree east of the Mississippi. While attempts to gauge its actual age have failed, the amazing tree is estimated to be somewhere between 500 and 1,500 years old. It stands 65 feet tall and the crown covers an area of

17,000 square feet. Its longest limb is 89 feet long. The Civil Rights advocate, Septima Clark, told stories of how Black families would often congregate under the Angel Oak's enormous branches to pray or picnic during the dark days of segregation.

Josh and Zach arrived at the Academy about 10:00, so they could get a training session in before the party started. Zach had been working with the six German Shepherds from Georgia since they arrived. The dogs had already been socialized and received basic obedience training prior to being delivered to the Academy. Because all TSA dogs operate under the same set of verbal and hand commands, the first few days of training were focused on teaching them these commands as well as allowing them to develop a level of trust of Zach as their handler. Nick was pleased with the professional way Zach interacted with the new dogs.

The three men met briefly to review the timetable for accommodating the TSA's eight-week delivery deadline. Nick asked Zach how the dogs were coming along with the commands.

"Very good," he answered. "Need to spend the rest of this morning on bark control."

Nick turned his attention to Josh. "How are you doing with Champ and Bullet?"

Josh nodded. "They're both good to go. Just fine-tuning the next few days."

Josh and Zach spent the rest of the morning working the dogs. Isaiah Robinson showed up around noon, and Nick helped him clean the kennels and feed the dogs before driving back to Charleston to get cleaned up for Amy.

The Sunday traffic was light, and Nick made it back home in twenty minutes. As he was getting off the elevator, he saw Allen, dressed in workout clothes with a towel hanging from his neck, getting ready to open the door to his condo.

Allen had just put his key in his door when he heard Nick call to him. "Hey, Allen."

"Hi, Nick. Looking forward to this afternoon. Anything I can bring?"

"Just yourself. How's the condo coming?"

"Getting there. If you've got a minute, come on over, and I'll show you the place." Nick walked down to Allen's unit and followed him in. He certainly expected that Allen's condo would be nice, but he was blown away when he actually saw it. It was a three-bedroom corner unit that was much more spacious than Nick had expected. Allen's taste obviously ran toward modern. Floor-to-ceiling windows and lush white shag carpet gave the living room a bright, airy feel that was accentuated by a contemporary white leather sofa with matching chairs and simple but elegant smoked glass living and dining room tables. Nick got the feeling he had walked into some Silicone Valley dotcom corporate office rather than a condo living room. He glanced at several magazines fanned out on a coffee table with names like; *United States Cybersecurity, Cybersecurity News, Advance Computer Science, and Wired.* The kitchen was off to the right and offered the same open feel with top-end stainless steel appliances and smoked glass cabinets. Several large abstract paintings hung on the walls with a few more leaning against one wall waiting to be hung. To Nick, they looked like spilled paint, but he figured they were each probably worth more than he had paid for his truck.

Allen tossed his gym bag on the sofa, and after giving Nick a quick tour of the place, led Nick onto an iron-railed balcony that overlooked the Ashley River and the City Marina with its fancy power boats and yachts. To the left was a breathtaking view of Charleston Bay, Ft. Sumter, and the vast blue-green expanse of the Atlantic.

Nick could not help but compare Allen's place with his own, which was just a few doors down the sixth-floor hallway. While Allen's condo was truly amazing, Nick was much more comfortable in the small, one-bedroom loft he rented with its second-hand furniture and mundane view of the intersection of Lockwood Drive and US-17. "Wow, Allen. Your place is incredible, and what an awesome view!"

"Thanks, Nick. I was lucky to find a place like this considering how fast the Charleston real estate market is heating up. Works out great for me. I love living downtown. Plus, I can ride my bike or walk to my office if I want to."

As Nick was leaving, he said, "Thanks again for showing me your place. I'll see you out at the Academy this afternoon. Planning on getting started about 2:00 or so."

"Great, Nick. See you then."

Back in his condo, Nick showered, shaved, and got dressed. He thought about Allen. He was an interesting guy, and he liked him. A bit standoffish about what he did for a living, but he was clearly good at it, considering his lifestyle. He knew Allen was a Charleston native and had spent time doing some sort of computer work for the government after he graduated from college, but not much more.

Nick put on a pair of tan Chinos, and then tried on several shirts before finally deciding on a tan, short-sleeve Polo with the insignia of his company's logo—the head of a German Shepherd embroidered over the words, "*The Academy.*" Nick looked at his watch and saw it was almost 1:30. He grabbed another company

Polo to give to Amy—figured it'd work better than flowers. He entered the coffee shop and saw Lisa, another barista. "Hey, Lisa, is Amy around?"

"She's in the back getting changed. I'm sure she'll be right out. Can I get you something while you wait?"

"No thanks," Nick said, just as the door to the ladies' restroom opened, and Amy appeared. She was wearing tight black jeans and a long lightweight gray cardigan over a lowcut V-neck white blouse that was highlighted by a simple leather and turquoise choker. This was not the Amy Nick was used to seeing during his early morning visits to The Cup. Her long black hair, normally drawn back into a ponytail, now hung well below her shoulders, and a hint of eyeshadow and lipstick gave her a softer, more feminine look.

Amy put on a pair of sunglasses, gave Nick an inviting smile, and said, "Hi Nick. All set?"

As banal as it sounded, Nick felt his heart skip a beat as Amy approached and he caught a hint of her perfume, subtle like spring rain. Nick held out the shirt and said, "Hi, Amy, a little gift for you. All set, I guess. You look sort of nice."

He couldn't believe how lame that sounded. *You look sort of nice?*

Amy's smile widened as she took the shirt and whispered, "Thanks, Nick. You look sort of nice, too."

They drove out to Johns Island with the windows down taking in the unusually cool and pleasant weather. Nick caught a glimpse of Amy, her head resting against the headrest, her long dark hair dancing in the wind. *Why'd you wait so long?* he thought.

Nick had just pulled his truck into the Academy's parking lot when he noticed a late-model Audi turn in right behind him. Allen got out of the Audi and called out, "Perfect timing!"

Nick and Amy joined him, and the three of them headed to the trailer. Josh, Zach, and Isaiah were inside helping Sally with the food, and after the introductions were made, Josh raised his beer to Amy and Allen and said, "Great you folks could make it. Amy, what can I get you to drink?"

"Thanks, Josh. White wine, if you have it."

"White wine it is. How about you, Allen?"

"Beer sounds great, thanks."

Nick got himself a beer and once everyone was settled, Nick proposed a toast welcoming Zach to the Academy. A few minutes later, Nick took Amy's arm and said, "Come on, I'll show you around."

Walking to the kennels, she asked, "Are the dogs you train here safe to be around? Police dogs look pretty scary to me."

"Good question, Amy. The dogs we train are around one-year old. We only have German Shepherds, and they tend to be fairly aggressive to strangers. That's why we only let our dogs 'off leash' when one of us is working with them. You definitely don't want to be bitten by a German Shepherd. Their bite pressure is 240 pounds per square inch, and that's higher than a pit bull's bite!"

"My sister, Cora, and I always had dogs when we were growing up in Mt. Pleasant," said Amy and then smiled. "Next time I see my mom, I'm going to ask her if she knows what her beagle's bite pressure rate is."

"You know, Amy, we live with dogs every day, but most of the time we don't give a second thought about the incredible things they can do. I get invited to a lot of schools to talk to the kids about training police dogs. It's funny. When I explain to teenagers that a dog has about 300 million olfactory receptor cells in their nose, which is about 50 times more than we have, they'll just shrug. Then I'll tell them that dogs can smell a hamburger three blocks away through traffic and exhaust fumes, and suddenly, I've got their attention." Nick laughed and said, "Then I really get their attention when I tell them that one of my drug-sniffing dogs can find a single marijuana joint in a warehouse full of tobacco!"

"Yeah, Nick, they are pretty amazing, but I see those military dogs on TV with our troops over in the Middle East, and it seems like all they do is work. That can't be fun for them."

Nick shook his head. "Actually, it's just the opposite. That's when our dogs are having fun. That's what they're trained to do, and it's like a game to them. If they make their handler happy, they're happy. Trainers always say, 'Give your dog a job. He'll give you his life.'"

"Well, I think is amazing what you do, and it seems like it's really rewarding."

"Definitely," Nick said, as he noticed another car pulling into the parking lot. "That must be Angela." Nick and Amy were out past the kennels when they saw Angela pull into the parking lot in an old Honda Civic. By the time they got back to the trailer, Angela had already introduced herself to everyone, and Josh was getting her a glass of wine.

Angela gave Amy and Nick a hug. "Wow, Nick, this place is cool, and it's a lot bigger than I pictured."

"Thanks, Angela. I'm glad you could make it. Hope your mom wasn't too upset with you leaving church early."

"Not at all. There's plenty of folks that can drive her home after the service."

"Great, I'll get the grill fired up. Josh, why don't you and Zach show Angela and Allen around. Isaiah, go ahead and give Sally a hand with the food. Let's plan on eating around 3:30 or so." Nick had to smile, as he watched Zach and Angela walk across the field toward the kennels. Zach was over a foot taller and almost 150 pounds heavier than Angela, but Nick's money would definitely be on Angela when it came down to who would be the boss in that relationship.

The set of speakers Nick had mounted on the side of the trailer filled the cool afternoon air with Creedence Clearwater Revival, Lynyrd Skynyrd, and ZZ Top. Sally's homemade potato salad and Angela's skewers of grilled okra complemented the hot dogs and burgers grilled to perfection by Josh, who was adorned in his Wolfgang Puck chef's apron and hat.

The bright sunshine and cool breezes made for a relaxing and laid-back afternoon filled with good conversation, horseshoe tossing, and games of frisbee interrupted periodically by Isaiah's stories about some of the strange and entertaining characters who called Johns Island home.

It was approaching 6:30 by the time the party started to wind down with everyone pitching in to clean up. Sally was the first to leave, volunteering to drop off Isaiah on her way home. Allen told Nick what a great time he had before heading back to Charleston in his Audi. Zach and Angela had spent the entire afternoon together, and it took some doing before Josh was finally able to drag Zach away. Angela was the last to leave. Nick and Amy waved goodbye to her as she pulled out and headed back to North Charleston.

"Come on, Amy, you can give me a hand. I need to check on the dogs and lock up the kennels."

Walking toward the kennels, Amy looked up at the wisps of gossamer clouds floating in an ocean-blue sky. "What a wonderful afternoon," she said. "I really enjoyed getting to know Sally, Josh, and Zach and would love to hear more of Isaiah's stories." A sly smile spread across her face. "And I think big Zach was smitten with Angela."

"You're probably right, Amy. He's a big guy, and I think he's got a big heart, too. He had a tough time over in Afghanistan, but I think he'll be okay. It's the way he acts around the dogs that gives me hope."

Amy slipped her hand through Nick's arm and, in a soft voice, said, "Tell me if I'm out of line, Nick, but Angela told me you had some pretty tough times yourself when you were a police officer, and it looks like your dogs played a big part in bringing you around."

Nick was caught off guard. He'd stayed away from talk of the specific details of the shooting and the extent to which it had messed up his life. Granted he had told Angela he left the police department because he'd been shot, but he didn't elaborate. After a somewhat awkward silence, Nick attempted to lighten things by saying, "Yeah, dogs are an important part of my life, but you know what they say, 'If you lock your wife and your dog in the trunk of your car for an hour, and then open it up…who's happy to see you?'"

Amy frowned. "I'm sorry, Nick. I didn't mean to pry. It's just that I read about what happened to you, and I think you've…well,

I think…well, I don't know what I think. I'm sorry. I'd better just shut up, now."

Nick stopped walking and turned toward Amy. "Don't worry. That was a pretty dark time in my life, and I had a lot of help working my way through it. Wait a minute. You said you read about what happened to me. Where?"

Amy, somewhat recovered from her embarrassment, gave Nick a wink and said, "I Googled you. There were a lot of Post & Courier articles about what happened back then. I can't believe what you went through."

"Like I said, I had some good people around me. I doubt I'd have made it without them." Nick didn't know the details surrounding Amy's divorce and didn't feel comfortable asking her about it on their first date. They'd reached the main kennels, and wanting to change the subject, Nick told Amy the names of the dogs and what they were being trained for while he checked to make sure they had enough water. He did the same with the six new dogs in the temporary kennels before walking back to the office to clean up.

The sun had set and light was fading by the time Nick and Amy left the Academy. It was a short fifteen-minute drive across the Johns Island Connector to her apartment on James Island. He parked the truck and when they reached her door, Amy pulled her keys from her purse and said, "Thanks for today, Nick. I had a great time." She gave Nick a quick kiss on the cheek and turned toward her door.

Nick touched her arm and said, "Amy, I was wondering if you would like—"

Before he could finish, Amy turned back, gave him a soft kiss on his lips, and said, "Yes I would."

CHAPTER NINETEEN

MAX DIMARCO'S CELL phone rang. He frowned when he saw the number and answered it with a curt, "Yeah."

There was a marked silence for a few seconds before a voice on the other end muttered, "We've got a problem."

DiMarco listened intently for the next few minutes, and then simply said, "I'll take care of it." He disconnected the call and sat quietly at his desk weighing his options.

CHAPTER TWENTY

THE CUP WAS crowded Monday morning, and Amy was behind the counter, busily taking orders when she saw Nick waiting in line and waved. She gave him a coy smile and said, "Well, good morning, Mr. Giordano. You're looking sort of nice this morning."

Nick laughed and said, "I get the feeling I'm never going to live that one down."

"Seriously, Nick, thanks again for yesterday. It was a perfect day."

"You're welcome. Hey, I thought if you're free later we could grab a sandwich at AC's. What do you think?"

"I'd like that. I've got a class until around 5:30, but I can meet you afterwards."

"Sounds great. I'll see you there." He picked up his muffin and coffee, saw Angela and Allen seated at a table by the window, and walked over to join them.

Allen slid a chair out for Nick and said, "Morning, Nick. Angela and I were just talking about yesterday. You've got a real nice operation out there, and we really enjoyed meeting everyone. But, I got a problem."

The concern was evident on Nick's face. "What's happened?"

Allen laughed and said, "You gotta help me. I can't get Angela to stop talking about her new best friend, Zach."

She shook her head and said, "Oh Lordy, that boy's a whole lot of man! I'm having him over to the house tomorrow for dinner. Mama wants to check him out."

They all chatted for a few more minutes until Allen looked at his watch and said, "Gotta run. Come on, Angela, I'll walk you to work. Have a good one, Nick."

Nick finished his coffee and left for the Academy.

No one had noticed the man in the gray sweatshirt watching them from a few tables away.

~~~~

The cold front had held, and the morning was clear and crisp. Allen left Angela at the entrance to Mercy General's emergency room but not before asking her if she could meet him after work at The Cup. He explained he was writing some programs for Mercy General and had some questions about the hospital. Angela said she'd be happy to do what she could to help and could meet him at 5:30. Allen thanked her and continued down Rutledge pass Colonial Lake to Queen Street.

Fifteen minutes later he arrived at his office completely unaware that he'd been followed. Standing in the shadows across the street from Allen's office, the man in the gray sweatshirt removed a cellphone from his pocket, dialed a number, and said, "Done." He listened for another moment and said, "Yes, sir."
~~~~

~~~~

Sarah was at her desk when Allen reached the top of the stairs and opened the door to his office. "Good morning, Sarah."

"Morning. There's some phone messages and a few checks for you to sign on your desk."

"Okay. Give me about ten minutes to get settled, and then let's review where we stand on the Rennells case." Allen set the phone messages aside, signed the checks, and booted up his computers. A few minutes later, he called Sarah into his office. "Any luck with the security footage?"

"Not really. Although, I'm getting familiar with the people who work there and what they do. Also, I've got a good idea of the process they use to receive different kinds of deliveries."

"What about how they handle drug and nondrug deliveries?"

"There's definitely a difference. Most of the deliveries are general stuff you would expect. You know, food, paper products, medical equipment, supplies. Stuff like that. These deliveries are taken to a large staging area where the delivery is checked against the order. There are usually two guys responsible for unloading and checking the actual orders against the purchase orders. There's another two fellows that separate the stuff and get it ready to send it to wherever it goes in the hospital. The whole thing is pretty much what you'd expect in a typical shipping and receiving department."

"All right, what about receiving the deliveries of drugs? How's that different?"

"From what I've seen," Sarah said, "it looks like they receive one regular delivery of narcotics each week on Friday afternoon from a company called Franklin Pharmaceuticals. I checked them out, and they're a big distributor of pharmacy products, mainly
~~~~

narcotics. They have a warehouse in Summerville. The same two employees who unload the regular trucks unload the Franklin truck, but the narcotics go directly into a separate room to be unpacked and checked. The room has two security cameras that monitor and record everything. You can tell they're drugs because they come in big bins that are sealed with colored plastic ties. Once they take the bins to the room, the two guys cut the ties and check the delivery against a purchasing order. They both sign off on the drugs before they reseal the bins with new ties and deliver them to the pharmacy."

"Okay," Allen said. "What about Federal Express shipments? Are they handled the same way?"

"Yes. You could tell the FedEx deliveries that had narcotics because they were taken to that same room, and I watched them being checked in the same way as the large drug deliveries."

"So, I'm assuming you didn't see any drugs disappear."

"Right, I watched the whole process three consecutive Fridays, and everything looked to be on the up and up. If any of those drugs are being taken, I sure didn't see it."

"So, you're saying the drugs seemed to be secure from the time they were unloaded to the time they were resealed and sent to the hospital pharmacy. Right?"

"Right," said Sarah.

Allen sat there for a while and then finally said, "Well, I still don't buy it. The only other place the drugs could be taken is in the pharmacy itself, and I just don't see it. I'll go ahead and download the security camera files from the pharmacy and review them myself. But I'd also like you to take another look at the footage from shipping—especially in that room where the drugs are taken to be inventoried against the order."

Sarah seemed a bit frustrated but said, "I'll do it. Did you come up with anything new on Friday?"

"I think so. But first, let's back up so we can get an idea of the volume of drugs we're dealing with. I was able to access the hospital's weekly purchase orders of pain pills and other forms of pain-related drugs. Believe it or not, the average weekly order for pills containing opioids approaches 10,000 pills. That's only pills and doesn't account for orders of other types of controlled substances or prescription drugs.

"I went back a few years and the profit margins for the hospital pharmacy have fluctuated less than one percent over that time. That drop of four to five percent in pharmacy's margin has got to mean a good chunk of drugs delivered to the pharmacy must be disappearing. Remember that these opioid pills can have a street value of ten to thirty dollars, if not more. That's somewhere between $10,000 and $30,000 for every 1,000 pills! And that doesn't include other pain medication! We're looking at some serious money here. I figure we could be looking at a street value of eight million dollars, if not more!"

Allen let that sink in and then continued. "Okay, so last week we learned that Chris Davis' health issues were related to his kidneys, and the problem was most likely caused by his ingestion of ethylene glycol. But we still don't know how the chemical got in his system.

"We also know we now have three more players in the mix; Kate Parker who temporarily replaced Davis in purchasing, Ken Tanaka, the Chief Pharmacist at PharmaTech, and Brad Strickland in shipping. I didn't find anything unusual in their personnel files, but I need to do some more in-depth vetting of their backgrounds."

Allen pointed to the phone number he'd written on one of the whiteboards and brought Sarah up to speed on the search he did on Chuck Thompson's direct phone line.

Sarah asked, "Did you check to see if that number showed up on any other phones inside the hospital."

Allen admitted he hadn't checked, but told her he would definitely run another search to see if anyone else at the hospital had made or received a call showing the number. He then explained his discovery of the $7,500 monthly withdrawals Thompson had made from his bank account and the likelihood that he had a serious gambling problem.

Allen continued, "From what you saw, the drug orders received in shipping seem to match the drugs orders issued by purchasing. And, if we can't find a problem in the pharmacy itself, then how do you explain the margin problem? You can't. These drugs aren't just vanishing into thin air, somebody has to be taking them."

Sarah said, "You were talking about a thousand pills. It wouldn't be hard for one of the shipping guys to hide those pills in his pants or somewhere and just walk out with them."

"You might be right, but the guys in security make frequent random checks of all the people who work in shipping and the pharmacy. They also random-check nurses and other hospital personnel. If anyone's doing that, they'll eventually get busted."

Sarah ordered sandwiches from Brown Bag Deli and spent the afternoon reviewing security footage from the shipping department. Allen did the same with the footage he downloaded from the pharmacy cameras. He was convinced that clues to the missing drugs were buried somewhere in those files.

Both Allen and Sarah came up empty-handed. A bit before 5:00, Allen shut down his computers and left the office to meet Angela at The Coffee Cup.

CHAPTER TWENTY-ONE

ANGELA WAS JUST walking into The Cup when Allen arrived. They both ordered iced lattes and made their way to one of several open tables. "How was your day?" she asked.

"Uneventful. I'm sure an emergency room is a lot more exciting than sitting behind a computer screen all day."

"Well, it does have its moments, I guess. Pretty quiet today, though."

"Have you always worked in the emergency room?"

"No. I started in pediatrics after I graduated. That was fun. Spent some time in cardiology and oncology. Oncology was the hardest. Then I was a 'floater' for about a year before I landed in emergency."

"What do you mean, 'floater?'"

"Oh, sorry. That means I was available to go to whatever department that needed the most help. I enjoyed that. I was able to help all kinds of patients."

"Sounds interesting. I imagine you got to know a lot of people who worked there." Allen took a sip of his latte before he continued. "Nick told me you've worked at the hospital since he's known you, and, to be honest, that's the reason I wanted to meet with you today. A better understanding of Mercy will help with the work I've been hired to do."

"Yeah, been there almost eight years, now. I guess I can help. What kind of work are you doing for the hospital?"

Now Allen needed to make a decision. How much should he tell her? He could use the cover story Rennells gave him about the security of patient records, but he knew he'd eventually need to ask her about drugs. Angela was definitely in a position to provide critical information about the informal practices relating to the use of narcotics he may not be able to secure otherwise. He'd only known her a few weeks. Could he trust her to keep their conversations confidential? Allen had to quickly weigh the value of the information he might get from Angela, with the possibility that his covert investigation might be somehow exposed. Allen lived in a world made up of ones and zeros. He lived in a world based on logic, and his years of government work at CERT had taught him to make decisions based on the logic of technology. Now he had to make a decision based on intuition.

He was lost in his head until Angela said, "Hey, Allen. Thought I lost you there. I said what are you doing for Mercy."

"Sorry. I must have zoned out." He made his decision. "I'm doing some confidential work that has to do with the use of drugs in the hospital."

Angela's smile disappeared the moment Allen said "drugs." It was as if a door that had been opened was slammed shut. "Look it, Allen, I'm not sure I want to get involved in this. I've been there a long time, and I've got a good reputation. I really need this job, and I don't intent to rat out any of my friends."

Allen had expected a reaction like this. He put his hand on her arm and quickly said, "No, that's not what I'm asking. This is completely different. Just give me a second to explain, and if after you hear me out, you want nothing to do with it, you won't hear another word about it from me. I promise."

"I like you, Allen. But the whole subject of drugs is a really sensitive area. I'm not going to get into who I think's using."

"That's not what I want, and I would never ask you to do that, Angela. I said this is different. Mercy has a problem, and I'm not talking about anyone using at the hospital. I'm talking about millions of dollars of drugs finding their way onto the streets of Charleston. Drugs in our neighborhoods and schools, and there's a chance some of those drugs are coming from Mercy. I can't tell you more than that. All I'm asking is that you trust me, and help me find out what's going on."

Angela just stared at Allen for a moment. She'd grown up in a neighborhood riddled with drug dealers and crime. She'd made it out, but many hadn't. Two of her closest high school friends died from heroin overdoses. "All right, first tell me what it is you want, and then I'll decide if I want to get involved, but remember, I'm not going to turn on my friends."

"Understood. The person who hired me has reason to believe that there may be one or more people at Mercy involved in an ongoing scheme to steal substantial amounts of drugs from the hospital. It's my job to figure out if that is, in fact, happening. And, if it is, how it's happening and who's involved. Once there's solid evidence, he'll bring in law enforcement."

"Are you talking about Mr. Summerton?"

"No, not Summerton, but someone who's very important. That's all I can tell you at this point. Okay, why don't we do this? Let me give you some names of people that work at the hospital, and you can give me your general impression of them. I don't really need specifics, just the first thing that comes to mind. Remember, whatever you say stays with me."

"Fine. Go ahead."

"Charles Summerton."

"Don't see him much but seems to be a good guy. I think everyone likes him."

"Blake Fitzgerald."

"Thinks he's better than everyone. Sneaks around. Doesn't smile. Wouldn't trust him. Just an asshole."

"Russ Slean."

"Accounting guy. Don't know him."

"Chris Davis."

"Purchasing guy. Worked at the hospital a long time. I used to see him in the hospital exercise room. Nice guy. I heard he got sick."

"Kate Parker."

"The bitch." Angela laughed. "She's been in purchasing forever. Thinks she knows everything. Thinks she runs the department. No one wants to mess with her."

"Ken Tanaka."

"Don't really know him. Seems nice, though. He came with the company that took over the pharmacy."

"Chuck Thompson."

"He's the shipping guy. Hear he just quit. Don't know him well, but supposed to be a nice guy."

"Brad Strickland."

"Don't know him."

"Great, Angela. That helps," Allen said. "Let me ask you this. Have you noticed anything different on the availability of pain medication over the last six months?"

Angela thought for a moment. "Not really. Seems like the emergency room doesn't have as big a stock of the stuff as before, but I imagine that's due to the new company that's running the pharmacy."

"Angela, I really appreciate your help. I have some ideas about what might be happening, but I haven't been able to nail anything down. I'll probably have more questions for you as I get deeper into this thing. Okay with you?"

"All right, just remember to keep my name out of it."

"Will do. Now, tell me more about this Zach guy you invited to dinner." Angela and Allen talked a few more minutes before saying their good-byes and heading home.

~~~~

At no time during their conversation had either of them noticed the man in the gray sweatshirt sitting several tables away. He wore earbuds attached to an iPhone, and he looked to be listening to music while he sipped his coffee. In reality, the device was not an iPhone but rather an ultrasensitive recorder capable of clearly capturing conversations up to one hundred feet from the source. Allen and Angela's entire conversation had been recorded.

The man in the gray sweatshirt was Angelo Vitale. He waited until both Allen and Angela left before he took out his actual iPhone and dialed Max DiMarco. He told DiMarco of the conversation he'd just recorded.
~~~~

"Good," DiMarco said. "Download it onto a flash drive and bring it to me tonight. I have another job for you." He disconnected the call without saying another word.

DiMarco did not particularly like Vitale but found his special skills useful in certain situations requiring things to be "fixed." Vitale was an enforcer, and while he was proficient in a variety of weapons, he was partial to the knife—he was a cutter. Knives don't make noise—guns do, and the site of a knife in his hand could sent a very convincing message.

CHAPTER TWENTY-TWO

AS ALLEN AND Angela were leaving The Cup, Nick had just entered AC's and found an empty table in the back under a poster of Michael Jordan draining "The Shot," a last-second basket to beat Cleveland in the '89 playoffs. A few minutes later, Amy walked in and he waved her over.

When she got to the table, Nick held the back of her chair when she sat down. She arched her eyebrows and said, "Wow! I can't remember the last time a guy did that for me. I thought chivalry was dead."

Nick laughed. "Not dead. Probably on life-support, but not dead. How was your day?"

"All right, I guess. But I have to admit that working full-time *and* going to school is starting to get to me. But you don't need to hear me whine. How was yours, Nick?"

"Fine. How much longer before you finish school?"

"Less than a year. Really, it hasn't been that bad. I had my associates degree before I got married, so that helped."

The waitress arrived and Nick order a beer and Amy asked for a glass of Chardonnay. Nick knew little about her divorce and wondered if it was too soon to pry. Nevertheless, he decided to go for it.

"How long were you married?"

Amy seemed a little surprised at the question. "Almost five years."

He went ahead and tried for a little more.

"What happened?"

Amy smiled. "Well, I guess that's fair. I asked you about your past on Sunday. I'll go first, but then it's your turn. All right?" Nick nodded, and she took a sip of her wine before continuing. "His name was Paul." She laughed to herself and said, "Well, I guess it still is. Anyway, I met him when I was going to school. He was a lawyer and about five years older than me. I guess you could say it was a whirlwind romance. We got married about six months after we met, and everything was great for the first few years. We bought a condo on Daniel Island, and I started working as a teacher's assistant at the elementary school on the island. Paul was an associate at the law firm and expected to put in sixty or more hours a week. It was crazy. He'd work all day and then would have to take clients to dinner a few nights a week. I didn't mind it too much because I had my work at the school and spent a lot of time with my mom and sister, Cora. They both lived in Mt. Pleasant."

Amy took another sip of her wine, which gave Nick an opportunity to say that detectives in his department were often expected to work long and odd hours and how that put a strain on their family life.

"I can appreciate that," she said. "He'd been at the firm five years and kept telling me things would ease up when he made partner. Well, things obviously didn't ease up; they only got worse. It felt like he was gone almost every night, and then there was the drinking. I guess I should have seen it coming. He started getting home later and later, and when he did make it home, his clothes would be wrinkled, and he'd smell like a brewery. But I hung in there telling myself he would change. Then one afternoon I dropped off one of his suits and a few of his shirts at the dry cleaners. I was leaving the store when the owner called me back to the counter. He handed the shirts and suit back to me and told me I needed to take them somewhere else. I didn't understand until he told me to look in the pocket of Paul's suit. I couldn't believe it, but there it was—a bag of cocaine. I was so embarrassed.

"He came home drunk that night, and when I confronted him with the cocaine, he just laughed at me. He said it was no big deal, and I was acting like a prude. That's when I decided I'd had enough. I told him I was going to my mom's house and started to leave. He grabbed my arm, and I tried to push him away. Then he hit me. Well, it was more like a slap, but the next thing I knew I was on the floor, and my mouth was bleeding. I remember looking up at him. He seemed like he was in a daze. I was able to scramble to the door and get out. I didn't have my car keys or phone, but when I made it out of the building, I saw an older man who lived there, and he let me use his phone to call my mom.

"She picked me up and took me to one of those doc-in-a-box places. I had my lip stitched up and stayed up most of that night with my mom and Cora, trying to come to terms with what had happened to my life."

"Did you report him to the police?"

"No. I know I should have," Amy said. "The next week, I got a lawyer and filed for a no-fault divorce, so the court would waive South Carolina's normal one-year separation clause. The only problem was that I didn't have any money. Paul had taken care of all the finances, and being a lawyer, knew how to hide whatever we did have. I had to borrow money from my mom to hire the lawyer."

"You must have got a decent settlement because of all the things he did to you," said Nick.

"I thought I would, but remember, Paul worked for one of the largest law firms in Charleston, and he had all their resources. We couldn't prove he hit me because I never filed a police report. Heck, we couldn't even prove any of the other things he did. His lawyers even argued that the whole thing was my fault. They said I never supported him in his work and even argued we had a 'sexless marriage.' Well, he was the one with the loose zipper. I know he was having a lot of sex, just not with me!" Amy realized she was raising her voice and caught herself. "I'm sorry, Nick, I shouldn't be dumping all this on you."

"No, Amy, don't think like that. None of that was your fault."

"That may be so, but I just got to the point where I didn't want to fight it anymore. I just wanted it to go away. As far as the court was concerned, there weren't any real assets outside of the condo, and that was fully mortgaged. In the end, Paul agreed to reimburse my lawyer's fee, and I walked away with basically nothing. But that's okay. I got out, and that's all I really wanted."

Nick didn't know quite what to say but was saved when the waitress returned for their food order. Nick ordered a BLT and Amy got a shrimp salad. After the waitress left, Amy smiled and said, "Well, now you know my sordid past."

"The only thing sordid about your past is your ex. What's he doing now?"

"Don't care much what he's doing now, but I did hear he got fired from the law firm. I guess his drinking and carousing caught up with him. I honestly don't think about him much anymore. I've moved on. I figure things will settle down for me after I get my degree and start teaching." She went on to tell Nick she'd kept in touch with her friends at the elementary school where she used to work, and the school's principal wanted her to do her student teaching there. "If I do a good job, I'm pretty sure I can land a full-time teaching position there after I graduate."

The waitress brought their food, and neither said much while they ate. When they finished, they ordered coffee, and Amy broke a somewhat awkward silence by asking Nick how he ended up starting the Academy.

Now it was his turn to open up.

"Well, dogs have always been part of my life. I can't remember when we didn't have one growing up on the farm in Killian. When I joined the police department, I worked hard to qualify for the K-9 Unit. It was a pretty coveted job and definitely not easy to get. As far as the Academy goes, it was actually my dad's idea, and there's no way I could have done it without his help." Nick actually felt himself choking up when he mentioned his dad. "Hell, there's no way I'd be sitting here right now if it hadn't been for my dad."

Amy picked up on this and gently put her hand on his. "Your dad sounds like a great guy."

"Yeah, he really is. I spent a year with him at the farm getting my life back together after I left the department." With the exception of Dr. Bailey, Nick hadn't opened up to anyone about the depths to which he'd fallen after the shooting—not even to his dad. He somehow felt different around Amy—he didn't know how to explain it other than he felt "safe" with her. For the next half hour, Nick talked about the shooting and its aftermath. He told her of the physical and psychological pain that led to his drinking. He told her how close he'd come to losing it all and how his time at the farm and his sessions with Dr. Bailey had brought him back from the edge. "I don't take things for granted anymore. I'm not saying I've forgotten how bad it was. I still wrestle with some of the things I did and the people I let down. But I try not to dwell on the past. Things are good now." He smiled at Amy. "Things are really good now."

"Sounds like we've both put our past behind us."

It was approaching 7:30 when they left AC's and made the short walk down King Street to the student parking lot where Amy left her car. She slipped her arm through Nick's, and neither said a word as the blue-gray shades of night descended on the Holy City. When they reached the parking lot, Nick leaned against her car and pulled her close. They just held each other until Amy looked up into Nick's eyes and whispered, "Thanks for everything." She gave him a soft kiss before pulling away to get her keys. "See you in the morning at The Cup."

Nick smiled. "Yes, you will." He watched her pull out of the lot and turn up Calhoun toward the James Island Connector. He made the short fifteen-minute walk to Bee Street, wondering if he might have just found that missing piece.

CHAPTER TWENTY-THREE

ANGELO "ANGEL" VITALE was not a big man. He was fairly nondescript with a few noticeable exceptions, the most prominent being the black tattoo of an angel on his right forearm. His jet-black hair was combed straight back into a ponytail, and his pockmarked angular face showed the remnants of what must have been a severe case of adolescent acne. There was a darkness about him.

He started running with the wrong crowd in his early teens in Cleveland. Once, a fellow gang member told him that not all angels were benign messengers of God, but there were also "avenging angels" sent to earth by God to carry out his judgments through violence. Angel liked that and had the tattoo of an avenging angel inked on his arm.

Angel removed the flash drive from the pocket of his gray sweatshirt and placed it on the desk in front of Max DiMarco. DiMarco inserted it into his computer, and for the next twenty minutes, the two men listened intently to the recorded conversation between Allen and Angela.

"We need to put a stop to this before it gets out of hand," DiMarco said when the conversation ended. "My contact tells me this Miller guy is some sort of computer whiz who's messing around with Mercy's files. If he figures out what we're doing at the hospital, all the rest of our operations could be jeopardized. I want him stopped."

Angel leaned forward. "Are you telling me you want him stopped—like permanently?"

"No, not yet. I don't need the cops sticking their nose in this. Just see if you can scare him off. I'll leave the specifics up to you. Go ahead and use that nurse if you want to."

"All right," Angel said, "but there's also another guy who might know something. I've seen Miller and the nurse meet this other guy at the coffee house. I don't know if—"

"Don't bother me with details. Just do whatever you need to do to make this thing go away," DiMarco ordered. "The hospital operation is profitable, but I'll shut it down if I have to. I got too much at stake. Now get out of here and do what you need to do, and do it quickly."

CHAPTER TWENTY-FOUR

THE NEXT MORNING, Allen and Sarah continued the tiresome job of reviewing the hospital's security footage. It was almost noon when Sarah stuck her head in Allen's office and said, "I think I found something. Not sure what to make of it, but come on out, and I'll show you."

Allen left his office and joined Sarah at her desk.

"Show me what you got," he said.

"It was right in front of me all the time. Just didn't notice. Watch this." Sarah had queued up footage from inside the shipping room used to check narcotic deliveries. "This shows last Friday's Franklin Pharmaceutical delivery." Sarah smiled. "Watch this, and tell me if you see anything strange."

She hit play, and the footage showed two workers carrying six narcotic bins into the room and locking the door. One of the men cut the plastic ties on the bins while the other man slid coins into a vending machine against the wall and pulled out what looked like a bottle of Coke. He put the bottle on the end of the table and said something to his partner, who then looked directly into one of the security cameras and scratched the back of his head. He then took some coins from his pocket but dropped them on the floor. Both men disappeared under the table to retrieve the coins and then reappeared a second later. The second man walked to the vending machine, got himself a bottle of Coke, and then both proceeded to inventory the drugs. Sarah stopped the footage and turned to Allen. "Well, what was wrong with what we just saw?"

Allen shook his head. "I didn't see anything unusual."

Sarah was clearly enjoying herself. "I'll give you a hint. Watch what the man does right before he puts his hand in his pocket. Also, what's missing?"

Allen looked confused and muttered, "Show it to me again." Sarah requeued the file. Now, Allen was getting frustrated. "Okay, so the guy scratches his head, both guys disappear under the table, then they come back out. I don't get it. Just tell me."

Sarah backed up the file to the first man getting his Coke from the vending machine. "Now, watch the soft drink." She played the file. The Coke the man put on the end of the table vanished the instant the two men reappeared from retrieving the dropped coins.

"Jesus!" Allen said. "Where'd it go?"

She backed the file up again. "Wait," she said. "There's more. Now, watch the timestamp on the upper right corner."

"Sarah, you're amazing! Almost four minutes. We're missing about four minutes on that footage. It shows those two guys missing for only a few seconds, which isn't long enough to activate the motion detector shut off."

Sarah and Allen then checked the two previous Franklin Pharmaceutical Friday deliveries. In both cases, one guy scratched his head right before both shipping employees disappeared from the screen for what looked like just a few seconds before reappearing. In both cases the timestamp on the screen jumped forward between three and four minutes.

Sarah shook her head and said, "So, now we know when the drugs are being taken, but where did they go, and how were both these security cameras frozen at that specific instant?"

"Think about it," Allen said. "Someone had to be watching those guys in the room. He sees the signal—the one guy scratching the back of his head—and freezes the cameras at just the right instant to give them enough time to remove the drugs from the bins. The guy must switch the cameras back on after the drugs are taken from the bins. It's got to be someone with access to the security camera system and the computer smarts to hack into it."

"Exactly," Sarah said. "You said these cameras are motion activated, so regular security guys monitoring the cameras probably wouldn't notice anything out of the ordinary, unless they're really concentrating on the timestamp. There's got to be twenty to thirty hospital cameras running at once, so there's no way they're going to notice a small change in the timestamp on the two shipping room cameras!"

Allen nodded in agreement. "That means at least three people have to be involved—the two shipping guys, and someone who really knows their way around computers. But if the drugs are being stolen during that three to four-minute gap, we still don't know where they go or how they're taken out of the hospital."

"Those shipping guys could be hiding the drugs on them and just walking out after work." Sarah suggested.

"Maybe," said Allen, "but we talked about that. This has been going on for almost six months, and you'd think they'd have gotten caught with all the security checks. Let's stay with those camera files. I bet there's a clue in there somewhere."

Allen thought for a minute. "Wait, there's something else. We know there's paperwork that comes with the delivery that lists the specific drugs included, right? And when those two guys finish checking the delivery against the purchase order, they put that paperwork back inside the bins before they're resealed. You've got to figure the pharmacy is going to check the delivery against the same paperwork. So, if those guys are taking a good portion of those pills, the pharmacy will know they're missing."

Sarah smiled. "Not if those guys have a different set of paperwork that doesn't include the pills they took."

Allen was amazed. "It would be simple for someone to access purchasing's computers to find out what was ordered. These orders are all digitally sent, so they're right there in their computers. Whoever is freezing the cameras decides what he wants the guys in shipping to take and then gets them new paperwork that matches what the pharmacy actually gets. What a setup. It's so simple, it's beautiful! Sarah, grab your purse. I'm taking you to lunch. You nailed it today!"

After a relaxing lunch at McGrady's Tavern, Allen and Sarah returned to the office. Sarah continued to review the security footage looking for additional clues.

Allen had previously used Mercy's internal personnel files to check the backgrounds of those employees in the shipping department, as well as Kate Parker in the purchasing department, Ken Tanaka with PharmaTech, and Brad Strickland, who was temporarily running the shipping department. Appreciating how easy it would be for someone with even moderate computer capabilities to modify an employee's personnel file, Allen spent the rest of the afternoon developing detailed profiles of those individuals using external data sources. He couldn't find anything suspicious on Tanaka or Strickland. There was nothing of substance in Parker's background either, with the exception of the amount of debt she was carrying. Parker had taken on a second mortgage on her home in Goose Creek, but she seemed to be current on her monthly payments.

Allen's efforts paid off when he discovered that the two employees handling the narcotic shipments had minor criminal records. Their names are Logan Jefferies and Scott Evans. They'd both spent short stints in jail for theft, and one of the men even had an active warrant. Interestingly, though, none of this was in their personnel files.

Late in the afternoon, Allen decided to do a little more digging on the mysterious 843 number he'd written on the whiteboard. He'd previously downloaded only the calls made to or from Chuck Thompson's direct line. It took him another twenty minutes to bypass Mercy's firewalls and access the hospital's historical phone records. He needed an additional several minutes to complete the download of all the departmental calls within the hospital during the month prior to Thompson's resignation. Once the download was complete, another few minutes were required to run the filtering program to isolate the number.

It was worth the wait. The program filtered a total of six calls that were made to the number. All the calls came from the security department's phone number. *Bingo!* Allen thought, *I knew it. Our third person works in security.*

He told Sarah of his discovery. "The only person I previously checked out in the security department was the head guy, Blake Fitzgerald. I couldn't find anything on him, but Angela told me the guy was very secretive, and not many folks at the hospital trusted him. We're pretty sure one of the guys involved in the drug theft probably works in that department. Now I need to run profiles for the rest of the people working there."

Before today, Allen felt he was getting nowhere fast, but with Sarah's discovery, things were coming together. He felt like a ten-year-old who'd just found a treasure map. "Sarah, you did great today. I think I'll make you CyberTech Security's Employee of the Month!"

Sarah laughed and said, "Well, it's 5:30, and your Employee of the Month is going home."

Allen smiled. "I'm going to stick around for a while and get started on those profiles. Seriously, Sarah, you had an amazing day today."

"Thanks, Allen. Now, don't stay too late. See you tomorrow."

Allen went back into his office and identified all the employees currently working in Mercy General's security department. Not completely trusting the employee personnel files, he again began the mundane task of researching employees using information external to hospital files.

Allen quickly eliminated those hourly employees who acted strictly as security guards under the assumption that they didn't have the necessary level of computer expertise or direct access to the system's main computers. This left a handful of security personnel Allen deemed potential targets. Blake Fitzgerald had begun his career at Mercy as a cybersecurity associate before eventually rising to the position of Chief Security Officer. The cybersecurity operation consisted of six full-time employees. Jerry Shields was the cybersecurity manager and supervised three computer techs—Chuck Outland, Sam Sutter, and Mike Williams. The other two employees in cybersecurity were secretaries.

It was approaching 7:00 when Allen decided to call it a day. He would continue his vetting in the morning. He shut down his computers and was about to activate his office security alarm when he felt a sharp crack on the back of his head. A searing flash of light blazed behind his eyes before his knees buckled and he fell like a house of cards. Everything went black. He was out cold before his face smashed into the floor, splitting open his lower lip and loosening several teeth.

Angel Vitale calmly pocketed the blackjack and injected one milliliter of thiamylal sodium into the back of Allen's neck. He then went into Allen's office and began taking pictures of the whiteboards with his iPhone. After snapping several additional pictures of Allen's office and smashing two computer monitors, he grabbed the red marker and wrote "Back Off Asshole" on one of the whiteboards. Two minutes later, he was out of the office and calmly strolling up Queen Street.

Thirty minutes later, the effects of the barbiturate began to wear off. Allen felt disoriented as he regained consciousness. He felt an intense pain in the back of his head and the coppery taste of blood in his mouth. He pushed himself into a sitting position and touched the back of his head. It felt wet. He looked at his palm—glistening red—and felt the swelling and caked blood around his mouth. Then he saw the pool of blood on the floor and realized he was on the landing at the top of the stairs leading to his office. The door to his office was open. It was coming back to him now.

Once he was able to stand, he held onto the door as the room began to spin. His head felt like Tiger Woods had just smashed it with a driver. Finally, he was able to walk, and when he got to the door to his office, he saw the message: "Back Off Asshole."

Two of his computer monitors had been shattered. He sat in his desk chair a few minutes trying to make sense of what just happened. His head was throbbing and still seeping blood. He felt nauseous. He fumbled for his phone and called Sarah. No answer. He wasn't calling his parents. And there was no way he was bringing the police into this, at least not yet. There was no one else he could think to call, and then he remembered Nick had given him his number before last Sunday's party. He made the call.

At first, Nick didn't recognize Allen's voice—it sounded slurred as if he had been drinking. Allen muttered something about having fallen and hurt himself, but he wouldn't go into detail. "All right, where are you?"

"I'm at my office. Right next to Robert Lange Studios. 8 Queen Street."

Robert Lange Studios was the premier art gallery in Charleston, and Nick knew exactly where it was located. He told Allen to stay put. He'd be there in ten minutes.

CHAPTER TWENTY-FIVE

ALLEN HAD SOUNDED drunk on the phone. Nick hadn't known him that long, but he certainly didn't seem to be a heavy drinker. But, then again, you never know. Nick remembered his battle with the bottle. He shook his head and thought, *I really don't feel like babysitting a thirty-year-old lush.*

Nick pulled up in front of 8 Queen Street, left his truck in a "No Parking" zone, and headed up the stairs to Allen's office, taking two steps at a time. The door to the office was wide open, and Allen was seated at Sarah's desk holding a towel to the back of his head, his mouth bloodied. "Jesus, Allen. What the hell happened?"

"I fell."

Nick glanced around and saw the broken computer monitors and files and printouts strewn across the floor. Then he saw the whiteboard. Nick didn't say a word and gently inspected the back of Allen's head. Seeing the three-inch gash glistening with blood, he said, "All right, Allen. Whatever you say, but right now we need to get you to the hospital."

"Okay, just as long as it's not Mercy General," Allen muttered.

As they reached the door, Allen told Nick to wait and then punched in the code on the security pad, activating the alarm system before leaving the office. Nick got him into his truck and made the short drive to MUSC's emergency room.

It was approaching 9:00, and the waiting area was packed. Nick made a few more attempts to get Allen to tell him what really happened without luck. A half an hour later, Allen was taken back to a room, where an obviously overworked resident cleaned and stitched his head wound and the cut on his mouth.

A few minutes later, the doctor found Nick in the waiting room and asked him what happened to his friend. "Who knows?" Nick said, "He told me he fell."

The doctor said he wanted to keep Allen overnight for observation, but he refused. "Look, I don't know what really happened to your friend, but it's important that you get him somewhere where he can rest quietly. He's got a concussion and doesn't seem completely coherent."

"Thanks, doctor, I'll take care of him."

"Oh, and tell your friend he's lucky. I don't know what he took tonight, but if you find it, throw it away." Allen was discharged fifteen minutes later.

Once back in Allen's condo, Nick said, "So, tell me what happened."

"I told you, I fell."

"Bullshit, Allen. I saw what happened to your office. 'Back Off Asshole?' What the hell does that mean? I'm not leaving here till I find out what's going on." Allen shook his head and remained silent. Nick wouldn't let it go. "Look, I saw all that computer stuff in your office. It's pretty obvious you do more than—what was it you said—'write a few programs?'"

Allen had already brought Angela into his assignment, and he knew the more people involved, the greater the chance of something going wrong. But Nick used to be a cop, and he trusted him. Plus, considering his condition and what Nick saw at the office, he couldn't exactly cling to the story that he'd fallen. "Okay, Nick. Sit down and I'll tell you what I can, but I need your promise it stays confidential. People could get hurt."

Nick looked at Allen's bandaged head and face. "It looks like someone already got hurt. Listen, Allen, you can trust me, but I need to know what's really going down."

Allen began by telling Nick his history with CERT and his exceptional ability to penetrate virtually any computer system. He explained he'd been hired to investigate the possibility that narcotics were being stolen from Mercy Hospital, but he left out any mention of MediGroup and the fact that Jack Rennells had personally hired him. He told him Angela was aware of his assignment, but only in general terms. It took Allen thirty minutes to give Nick a general overview of what he and Sarah had learned, but again, he left out many specifics of the operation.

Nick didn't say a word until Allen had finished. "Any idea who attacked you tonight?"

"No, but it does tell me we're getting close to whoever's behind what's happening at the hospital."

Nick glanced at his watch and was surprised to see it was already after 11:00. "It's late, and the doctor told me you've got a concussion and need to rest. I'll check on you first thing in the morning, but now you need to get some sleep." Allen agreed to give Nick a key to his condo and the code to deactivate the security alarm.

"Nick, I can't thank you enough for tonight. I really appreciate it. Remember, what we talked about tonight needs to stay between us. Right?"

"All right. But we need to tell Angela what happened to you. She's part of it now, too."

Allen nodded his agreement. As soon as Nick left, Allen phoned Sarah and explained the basics of what had happened, leaving out any mention of his injuries. He told her to stay away from the office tomorrow. He would call her in the morning, and they would decide what to do next.

Allen took the Tylenol the doctor had given him, turned out the lights, and sat quietly in his living room trying to determine how best to proceed. He didn't know how his cover had been blown, but it was evident that his investigation was no longer covert, and whoever was behind the drug theft had sent a clear message tonight—"Back Off Asshole." Allen had no intention of backing off but realized the situation had just become much more dangerous—to make matters worse, he'd now exposed Sarah, Angela, and Nick to that danger. Allen was exhausted, but found it difficult to fall asleep, and it was well after 1:00 before he drifted off into a fitful sleep.

Nick also had problems settling down when he returned to his place. His mind was racing. His first reaction was to go to the police, but he'd assured Allen he would keep what he was told confidential. Like Allen, it was well after midnight before he found sleep.

CHAPTER TWENTY-SIX

NICK'S ALARM RUSTLED him out of bed at 6:00 the following morning. It was still dark out as he sat in bed trying to digest the events of the night before and then remembered he needed to check on Allen before he left for work. He quickly showered, dressed, and headed down the hall to Allen's apartment. He unlocked the door, entered the condo, and deactivated the alarm system. Allen was fast asleep in the same chair Nick had left him the night before. He covered Allen with a blanket he found in the bedroom, left a short note asking Allen to call him as soon as he awoke, and quietly left to get coffee at The Cup.

Amy wasn't working that morning, but he saw that Angela had already arrived and was sitting by herself. He ordered his coffee and muffin and walked to her table, wrestling with how to tell her what had happened to Allen the night before.

"Good morning, Nick," Angela said with a smile. "What's up?"

Nick remained silent for a moment then took her hand and said, "We need to talk."

Her smile immediately disappeared, and she turned to face Nick, "Oh God, what is it?"

Nick started to explain what had occurred the night before, beginning with the call he'd received from Allen. He told her the extent of Allen's injuries and the condition of his office, including what was written on the whiteboard. "I took Allen back to his condo after the doc sewed him up, and he told me what was really going on at the hospital. I know he talked to you about it, but you don't know the whole story." He then explained, as succinctly as possible, the extent of the drug situation at Mercy and the fact that Allen's investigation was now exposed. "Angela, if they know about Allen, then they probably know about you. I don't know what Allen intends to do about this, but we're both in the middle of it now. He was in pretty bad shape last night when I left him. I checked on him this morning, and he was still sleeping. I'll get ahold of him later, but let's plan on all meeting here after work."

Angela was stunned. "I can't believe this is happening. I told Allen I didn't want to be involved. Damn it!"

"I understand," Nick said. "Look, we're both in this now, so let's just meet with him and figure out what to do about it."

"All right, I'll be here after work."

~~~~

Nick and Angela left The Cup completely unaware that Angel Vitale, just like he'd done before, had recorded their entire conversation. He'd be back at the coffee shop later that afternoon to see if his efforts the night before had succeeded in putting an
~~~~

end to this pain in the ass investigation. He saw no reason to bother Mr. DiMarco until he had something more definite to report. DiMarco told him to handle it, and that's exactly what he intended to do.

CHAPTER TWENTY-SEVEN

NICK GOT TO the Academy at about 8:00, knowing he had a full day ahead of him. The people from Atlanta would be arriving about noon to pick up Champ and Bandit, and Nick needed to get them ready and make sure the paperwork was in order. He was also replacing Champ and Bandit with two new green dogs that would be delivered that day. Josh had his hands full making sure the balance of his dogs remained on schedule to meet their delivery dates. Zach continued to work with the six TSA dogs to meet the eight-week target date promised to the Department of Homeland Security. Sally had her normal duties keeping the whole place running smoothly, and Isaiah now had six more dogs to feed and cleanup after.

Despite his demanding work schedule, the events from the previous night remained foremost in Nick's mind throughout the morning. Allen finally called shortly before noon; he was at his office cleaning up the mess. Nick told him he had met Angela that morning and explained what had happened. Allen agreed they needed to meet and promised he'd be at The Cup that evening.

~~~~

As Allen hung up the phone, he heard a key unlock the front door and watched Sarah enter the office and shut the door behind her.

"Lock it," he said.

She did and then gasped when she saw his bandaged and swollen face. "Come on in to my office, and we'll talk." He turned, and she saw the bandage on the back of his head.

"Jesus, Allen. You didn't tell me you got hurt."

"Sit down, Sarah, and I'll explain. But first, that door stays locked, and I don't want you here anymore by yourself." He then told her about the attack and that his friends, Angela Martin and Nick Giordano, were now aware of their assignment. "It was my mistake. I should never have involved them, but it's done, so I'll have to deal with it. I don't know who's behind this or how much they know, but I don't want to expose you to what may happen and I have no problem if you want out."

She sat there trying to absorb how quickly and radically their situation had changed. "No, Allen, I'm not going anywhere. But, you're right, things are different now, and we can't take anything for granted."

"All right, but remember, I have no problem if at any time you want to back out. Agreed?"

"Agreed."

Allen admired her determination. It matched his own. "All right, then. I think the next step is to somehow put pressure on Thompson, and it may take me actually confronting him with what we know to get him talking. But leave that part to me. Remember, I don't want you here by yourself, and that door stays
~~~~

locked. And we both need to keep our eyes open when we leave the office. There's a chance we may have been followed."

They both worked the next few hours; Sarah reviewing the security footage and Allen continuing his vetting of Mercy's security personnel. They left together at 5:00. Nick walked with Sarah up Queen Street to Franklin. Her condo was a block up Franklin at the corner of Magazine Street, only a few blocks from the College of Charleston's campus where her husband, Dave, taught. Allen continued on to Colonial Lake and up Rutledge to Bee Street, arriving at The Cup at a shade before 5:30.

There were only a few customers in the shop, but Allen's bandaged face drew stares when he walked in. Angela and Nick were already seated at a table next to the wall separated from the other patrons. They wanted to take no chances their conversation might be overheard. They both seemed somewhat reticent when Allen joined them. "First, I want to apologize to both of you. Angela, it was selfish of me to bring you into this thing, and the same goes for you, Nick. I had no idea anyone had discovered what I was doing, but I should have known better."

"Who else knows about this?" Nick asked.

"Only my assistant, Sarah Pryor. I promise I won't involve you guys anymore."

"Well, that's nice of you, Allen," Angela said in a somewhat sarcastic tone. "But how do we know whoever attacked you last night won't try the same thing with us?"

"I understand, Angela, but I just don't know. What do you want me to do?"

Nick leaned forward and said, "Look, let's calm down. Let me ask you this, Allen. Assuming these people know we're involved, what are the chances they'll back off if you stop your investigation?"

Allen thought for a minute. "It's hard to say, but my gut says they won't leave it alone. They know they're exposed and probably have too much at stake to let it go, even if I stop."

"I suppose you're right," Nick said. "What about going to the police? Jesus, Allen, you just got your ass kicked, and your office was vandalized. They'd sure as hell do something about that."

"I know, but think about it. I never saw who attacked me, and you gotta figure that whoever did it was smart enough not to leave any clues. And as far as what's going on at Mercy—I've learned a lot but nothing solid enough to give to the cops, and they're not going to do anything without hard evidence."

"That's fine, but what about us?" Nick said.

"I know, but the reality is that unless I can actually prove who's behind all this, they're not going to stop. I just never should have involved you guys."

"The bottom line is we're involved," Angela said, "and these assholes are pushing drugs on our streets. I grew up around this shit and know if you let it go, it'll only get worse. Yeah, I'd rather not be part of this, but if I am, I'm not going to sit back and let them come after me without a fight. I've had to fight all my life, and I'm not stopping now!"

"I think Angela's right, Allen," Nick said. "None of us want this, but if we're in it, we need to know everything you know."

"All right, I'll bring you up to speed with everything I've got so far, and I promise I'll let you know what develops. I know I haven't handled this well, but all I ask is to give me a little more time."

Angela looked at Nick, and they both nodded. Allen brought them up to date with what they knew, how they discovered it, and what they needed to find out before the authorities were brought in. Like before, he made no reference to MediGroup or Jack Rennells. "Sarah and I'll continue analyzing the information I've been able to download from Mercy's internal files, but now that our investigation is no longer a secret, I need to start putting pressure on those people we think are involved. I'm going to confront Chuck Thompson and use his gambling problem as leverage to see if he'll talk."

Allen promised to let them know how it went with Thompson. The meeting broke up with Nick and Allen leaving together and Angela heading home to meet Zach who was coming over to have dinner with her and her mother.

~~~~

Angel Vitale couldn't believe the wealth of information he'd just discovered, and every word of it was recorded. What concerned him the most was the comment about pressuring Chuck Thompson. He always figured Thompson was a weak link and needed to be eliminated, but that was DiMarco's call. Either way, it looked like the little message he left the night before for this Allen Miller guy didn't take. He decided he needed to tell DiMarco what he'd just learned. Thompson had to be dealt with, but it needed to be okayed by DiMarco if the solution was to be permanent.
~~~~

CHAPTER TWENTY-EIGHT

ALLEN PHONED SARAH that evening and told her he planned on making an unannounced visit to Chuck Thompson in the morning, and she shouldn't come in to the office until he called her. He also let her know that he had let Angela Martin and Nick Giordano in on what they had learned. He would keep them informed of their progress, but he didn't want them directly involved in the investigation. He'd given them their office phone number and both their cells. Allen had Sarah copy down their cell numbers and the number to the Academy. He told Sarah to call Nick if anything went wrong.

Allen was up early the next morning. He was changing the dressing on his mouth and noticed the bruise on the right side of his face had turned a deep bluish-yellow. The swelling had gone down, but he knew the condition of his face would certainly affect Thompson when he saw him that morning. It was clear that Thompson had been pressured to leave Mercy because of his gambling problem, and Allen decided he'd approach Thompson as if he was part of whoever was putting the squeeze on him.

Chuck Thompson lived off the Glenn McConnell Parkway in West Ashley, a twenty-minute drive, depending on traffic. Allen drove his Audi A6 to Thompson's house, arriving at 9:15. A woman that Allen assumed to be his wife answered the door, and he told her he was from Mercy General and needed to talk to her husband. A moment later, Thompson appeared at the door. Allen had never seen Thompson but knew he was around forty and was surprised when he appeared at the door. He looked much older. He was obviously nervous—sweat dotted his upper lip.

"My wife said you're from the hospital. What do you want?"

Allen was quiet for a few seconds, allowing Thompson to take in the condition of his face and then said, "Chuck, we need to have a little talk. I suggest you come outside, so your lovely wife won't hear what I have to say."

"I don't know who you are, and I don't work at Mercy anymore. What do you want?"

"You're right, Chuck. You don't know me, but I know you. I know you don't run the shipping department there anymore, and I know why you left. So, like I said, let's talk outside."

Thompson turned around and saw his wife standing at the end of the hallway listening. He quickly stepped outside, shutting the door behind him. "Who are you, and what do you want from me?"

Allen stared at Thompson, seeing the fear and confusion in his eyes. "You don't need to know my name, Chuckie. Oh, and by the way, I'm not from the hospital. But I know what you did."

"I don't know what you're talking about."

Allen slowly shook his head. "Oh, I *bet* you do know what I'm talking about. You like to *bet*, don't you, Chuck. How's that working for you? Your luck change yet? And how's that savings account of yours? And where's that seventy-five hundred dollars? And don't fuck with me, Chuck."

"Okay, okay. Wait. I just don't have that much now, but I can get it. Just give me some more time." He looked back at his house and saw his wife standing in the front window staring at him. "Please, just give me some time."

"Sure, Chuck, we'll give you some time. You're a good guy. But first, tell me how you got the drugs out of the hospital."

Thompson looked surprised. "I don't know anything about that. You guys just told me to keep my mouth shut and look the other way. I did everything you told me to do. You told me to quit, and I quit. You promised you'd leave me alone. Please, I've got a wife and kids. You promised."

Allen now understood that Thompson probably wasn't directly involved with the theft. Whoever was pulling the strings, was just using his gambling debt as leverage to make him turn a blind eye to what was going on in his department.

"Who told you to quit, Chuck?"

Thompson looked confused. "Wait a minute. You're not one of Grasso's guys. Who the hell are you?"

"Who's Grasso?" Allen quickly asked.

Thompson now realized he'd been played. His face turned the color of a slice of watermelon and he scowled, "Get the hell out of here. I'm not saying another word!"

Allen knew he'd gotten everything he was going to get. "Thanks, Chuck, you have a nice day." He walked back to his Audi, pulled out of the driveway, and headed back to Charleston.

He phoned Sarah on his way and told her he'd meet her at the office.

Sarah was outside the office waiting for him when he arrived. When they got inside, he described his conversation with Thompson and wrote the name, "Grasso" on one of the whiteboards.

They spent the rest of the day in the office, Sarah reviewing the security footage, and Allen vetting the rest of the security department personnel. Later that afternoon, Sarah was watching the camera footage in the narcotics room when she paused the file and said, "Well, I'll be damned. I can't believe it. Allen, can you come out here a minute?"

Allen stuck his head out of his office. "What?"

Sarah pulled a chair next to her, patted the seat, and said, "Sit." Allen sat, and she continued. "I've been sitting here for hours staring at the camera shots of that room where the drug deliveries are checked. The cameras in this room are motion activated, so, obviously they're not filming when nobody's in the room. They check in the drugs there, but why else would anyone go into the room?"

Allen thought a moment and answered, "To take a break, I guess."

"Right, and what's the only other thing in that room?"

"The table and chairs."

"Yes, but what else?"

"The vending machine. So?"

"Right, again. I'm watching the camera switch on when the employees come into the room to get something to drink. They either leave or sit at the table until they finish their drink."

Allen nodded. "Okay. What are you saying?"

Sarah smiled. She was having a good time again. "The last three Fridays, right before 5:00, a guy from the vending company comes into the room to restock the machine and replace the container that holds the coins and dollar bills. We had vending machines at the school where I used to work, and I know the coin containers are sealed, so they can't be opened until they get back to the company. That's why the guy puts an empty one back in the machine. But then he looks around to see if anyone is watching, pulls out a second key, and opens a panel on the side of the machine. He pulls out a second container, shoves another one in to replace it, and then leaves with the two containers."

"Son of a bitch," Allen spouted.

Sarah's smile broadened. "So, Boss, what's in the second container?"

"Son of a bitch!" Allen repeated. "Those shipping guys put the drugs in that second container. Hell, who's going to check some vending guy? I can't believe it! Sarah, you're one wicked smart lady!"

"At first, I thought there might be a bottle opener on the side of the machine, and the second container was used to collect the bottle caps. But all the bottles are plastic and have twist-off tops. Then I thought maybe the second container had the computer stuff in it that operates the machine. But that didn't make sense— I remembered you've got to open the back of those machines to get at the controls."

"It's got to be how they get the drugs out," interrupted Allen. "You're right, I can't think of any other reason for the second container. It's easy enough to check. Go ahead and contact a few vending machine manufacturers."

"I will," said Sarah, "but, I say we assume it's how they get the drugs out. That means the vending guy is probably involved, and now all we need to know is where he's taking the stuff."

"It's Thursday, so if they keep the same schedule, that means there'll probably be another pickup tomorrow afternoon. You said the vending guy shows up late. Who knows if he's got other stops, but most likely it won't be long before he heads back to wherever he came from. I can just follow his truck."

Sarah seemed concerned. "That's cops and robbers stuff, Allen. You ever done anything like that before?"

Sarah had a good point. "No, the only time I've ever tailed anyone was on the internet. Plus, my Audi would stick out like a sore thumb. I suppose I could ask Nick if I could use his truck."

CHAPTER TWENTY-NINE

IT WAS AFTER 6:00 when Allen got back to his condo, and after dropping off his briefcase, walked down the hall to Nick's apartment. He heard music coming from inside the apartment and knocked. Nick looked through the peephole and was a bit surprised to see Allen's face. He pulled off the chain lock and opened the door. "Hi, Allen."

"Hey, Nick. Got a minute? I've got something to ask you. Hope I'm not interrupting."

"Not at all. Come on in." Nick grabbed his phone and turned off his Pandora app. "I just made some coffee. Can I get you some?"

"Do you have anything stronger?"

The comment got Nick's attention. He got a beer from the refrigerator and handed it to Allen. "Have a seat. You said you wanted to ask me something."

They both sat down in the small living room and Allen said, "First, I want to apologize again for getting you and Angela mixed up in this thing. I know she's really upset with me."

"What's done is done. I wouldn't worry too much about Angela. She's tough."

"I hope she didn't tell anyone about what's going on at the hospital."

Nick took a sip of coffee and said, "Not a chance. I know Angela, and if she told you she'd keep it on the down low, that's where it'll stay. So, what is it you wanted to ask me?"

Allen placed his beer on the coffee table and told Nick about the encounter with Thompson and Sarah's vending machine revelation.

"This guy services the machine every Friday afternoon, and I need to follow him to see where he goes. My car is a new Audi and probably a little too conspicuous. I wondered if I could borrow your truck. It would be just for a few hours."

Nick stared at Allen for a moment. "You ever done anything like that?"

"No, not really."

"I didn't think so," Nick said. "If this vending person is really doing what you think he's doing, he's going to be watching for a tail. He'll probably make you within a few minutes of leaving the hospital."

"Well, that's a chance I'll have to take."

"And what are you going to do when he gets to wherever he's going?"

"I'm not sure, yet. I'll figure it out."

Nick leaned forward and looked Allen in the eye. "Listen, I know you can do some amazing shit with your computers. But now you're talking about something completely different. Trust me. I lived in that world for years. You can't hide behind a computer out there."

"I know that, Nick. But I don't have a choice, do I?"

They were both quiet for a time, the silence growing heavy until Allen said, "I think I need another beer."

"Sure."

This gave Nick a chance to think. He returned from the kitchen with the beer and said, "I don't suppose I can talk you out of this. Can I?"

"No, I don't think so."

"If you're going ahead with this, you might as well do it right. I'm coming with you."

Allen shook his head. "Nick, I'm not asking you to do that. You're involved enough already."

"That's a little late. Don't you think? Now, tell me again what happens when the vending guy shows up."

Allen went over the whole thing again, Nick interrupting several times with specific questions. After about five minutes, Nick said, "Okay, give me tonight to think about this, but plan on getting back here around 2:00 tomorrow afternoon."

Nick stood to let Allen out, but Allen remained seated. After it became evident Allen wasn't going anywhere just yet, Nick sat back down. "Don't tell me. There's something else."

Allen smiled. "What are the chances of getting me some information about the loansharking players in Charleston?"

"Jesus, Allen. All right, explain."

Allen told him about Thompson leaking the name "Grasso" and that it was clear this Grasso fellow was the person Thompson had borrowed money from to cover his gambling debts. It also sounded like Grasso was wrapped up in the drug situation at the hospital.

"I still have good contacts at the department. I'm assuming you want this off the grid. Right?"

"Yes, just until we can get enough evidence to bring in the police."

Allen stood and was getting ready to leave when his cellphone began ringing. It was Sarah. He accepted the call and listened intently for a minute or so. "Damn. Okay, thanks for telling me." Allen disconnected the call, turned to Nick, and said, "Thompson's dead."

CHAPTER THIRTY

NICK WAS STUNNED. It took a few seconds to regain his composure. "Jesus, Allen. You were just with him this morning."

"Yeah, and he was definitely rattled when I left him. Sarah was watching the evening news and said the reporter called it a 'tragic event.' She didn't get all the details, only that a Charles Thompson was found dead late this morning in one of the parking lots at Citadel Mall. He'd been attacked with a knife and bled out in his car. Makes me think he probably knew whoever did it. The police are calling it a robbery/murder but had no further comment."

"Did anyone else see you this morning when you were at his house?"

"Yeah, his wife. She got a good look at me and probably saw my Audi parked in the driveway." Allen pointed to his bandaged mouth. "Hard to miss this."

"Do you think she might have gotten your license plate number?"

"No, I pulled straight into their driveway. Remember, South Carolina has only one plate, and that's in the back of the car."

"Any chance Thompson told his wife about your discussion?"

"I really doubt it. He'd drained their savings and was involved with some pretty nasty people. I bet he'd want to protect his family as much as possible. Jesus, Nick, do you think whoever's stealing the drugs had Thompson killed?"

"Looks that way, but this isn't the movies. Criminals don't run around murdering people left and right. It's bad for business. If someone did murder Thompson, that means this thing is probably bigger than we thought."

Nick opened the door to let Allen out. "Listen, I need to be out at the Academy early in the morning and probably won't get a chance to see Angela at The Cup. If you see her, tell her what happened to Thompson. I'll get ahold of one of my contacts in the department to see if they've got anything on this Grasso guy and let you know. Remember, be back here at 2:00."

CHAPTER THIRTY-ONE

THINGS AT THE Academy had grown even more hectic with the addition of the TSA dogs. Zach was doing a great job with the new dogs, but training six sniffers in a matter of only eight weeks was more than a one-man job. Nick was splitting his time between working with Zach and helping Josh stay on top of the other twelve German Shepherds. He had little time to spend in the office, and thank heaven for Sally who was once again working her magic with customers and suppliers.

Considering all the recent events, Nick was thankful Zach was staying close to Angela. He asked him how things were going with her, and all he could wrench out of him was, "She's a nice lady."

Later that morning, Nick took a break and was able to get ahold of Allen at his office. Allen said he did meet Angela that morning at The Cup and told her about Thompson's death.

"How'd she take it?" Nick asked.

"She's okay. Like you said, she's tough. She did tell me Zach's dropping her off in the morning and picking her up after work."

"Good. That makes me feel better. I've got to get back to the dogs. I'll see you at 2:00." Nick hung up and then put in a call to Steve Williams.

"K-9. Williams speaking."

"Steve, it's Nick. How's it going?"

"Nick, good to hear from you. Things are good. Chasin' the bad guys. Congratulations, heard you got the TSA order."

"Yeah, we did. Thanks again for all your help."

"Glad to do it. What can I do for you?"

"Well, I was wondering if you could check out something for me. There's this guy named Grasso who's supposedly involved with the loansharking racket in Charleston. I was hoping to find out more about him. Like maybe who he works for. Stuff like that."

The phone was silent for several seconds, and then Williams said, "I don't imagine you want to tell me what this is all about."

"No. I need you to trust me on this. I promise it won't come back on you. It's important."

"Okay. We don't get involved much in that area, but I'll make a few calls. Give me an hour or so."

"Thanks, Steve. I owe you one."

Around 1:00, Nick told Sally he had an appointment downtown and needed to leave early. The unusually pleasant weather of last weekend was gone, and temperatures were back in the 90s, with the humidity once again drenching the Low Country. "Sally, do me a favor and tell Josh and Zach to wrap it up early today. It's getting really hot out there, and we worked the dogs pretty hard today. Plus, we're supposed to get some afternoon thunderstorms."

"Will do. You go ahead, and I'll see you in the morning. Isaiah's coming out later this afternoon. I'll stay with him and close up."

"Thanks, Sally. You're the best." Nick left the Academy and was driving across the Johns Island Connector when Steve Williams called.

"Steve, any luck?"

"The short answer is yes. Grasso runs one of the biggest sharking operations in Charleston. I don't know why you're asking about this, Nick, but my best advice is to leave it alone. I talked to Rick Horton in vice, and he says they've been surveilling Grasso for a while. They've got him tagged as part of some bigger operation. Hell, the Feds are involved."

"Did you find out who Grasso's hooked up with?"

"No, they know he's connected but haven't been able to figure out with who, yet. The Feds suspect involvement with a syndicate out of Jersey. They're talking gambling, drugs, prostitution— the whole nine yards. Seriously, Nick. This is not something you want to be anywhere near. It's a snake pit."

"Thanks, Steve. I appreciate the information."

"Nick, did you hear what I just said? Leave it alone!"

"I'll be careful," Nick said, calmly. "I'm still only on the outside of this, but I'll let you know if I learn anything else."

"All right, but watch your ass on this one." You could hear the concern in Steve's voice.

Nick made a quick right onto Courtenay and pulled into his Bee Street parking garage a few minutes later. Once back in his apartment, he went to his bedroom closet and pulled down a shoe box. He laid it on his bed and hesitated before lifting off the top of the box and removing the Glock 21, which was wrapped in a heavy silicone cloth. Nick turned in his official handgun when he resigned from the department but purchased an identical one when he started his company. He appreciated its accuracy and light recoil and could count on the legendary stopping power of the .45 AUTO rounds with a ten-round magazine capacity. Nick rarely carried his gun but made a practice of visiting Charleston's Quick Shot Shooting Range once a month to maintain the "Marksman" ranking he'd achieved on the force. He slipped on his shoulder rig, covering it with a lightweight windbreaker.

Nick had just shut the door to his apartment when he saw Allen was also leaving his condo. Allen joined him, and they continued to the elevator without saying a word. Once in the elevator, Nick punched the parking garage button and said, "You ready for this?"

Allen noticed the bulge under Nick's windbreaker and saw the leather holster. "I'm ready, but there's something else."

"What?"

"I got a call from Angela about a half an hour ago. She was in the emergency room late this morning when an ambulance brought in Chris Davis. Angela was working with the attending physician who immediately diagnosed a heart attack caused by acute Stage 5 renal failure. His kidneys just shut down. Apparently, he's been going downhill for the past several months. He's been admitted, but he's in a coma. They've got him on dialysis, but the doctor thinks his heart isn't strong enough to make it."

"Christ," Nick said. "First Thompson, now Davis. I bet someone got to him."

"That's what I thought, but the emergency room doctor contacted Davis's nephrologist, who said his disease had reached the point where a heart attack was inevitable."

"Well, that's a hell of a coincidence. Isn't it? All right, let me tell you what I learned from my contact in the department. Apparently, your guy Grasso is a heavy hitter in the loansharking and blackmail business. This is mob stuff, and the FBI is involved. All I know is that where there's big money, there's big danger."

Things were happening too fast. They were both quiet for a moment as the enormity of the situation continued to sink in. Then Nick heaved a sigh and said, "Let's do this thing."

They left the garage and spent the next ten minutes cruising around Mercy General identifying the best location to monitor the hospital's shipping dock. There was a small parking area just north of the entrance to the dock that afforded a fairly clear view of the area. Nick pulled in and parked the truck. It was 2:25.

They sat in the truck for a time watching the dock without speaking. After about ten minutes, Nick noticed Allen fidgeting with his phone and could tell the pressure was starting to get to him. "Hey, Allen, what are you up to when you're not doing your computer thing? Any hobbies?"

"I run," he answered. "Nothing competitive. As you can imagine, most of my day is spent behind a computer, so I just enjoy getting outside. There was a group of us that would run together when I was working in Washington. How about you?"

"Played a lot of hoops and baseball in high school. Never good enough to play college ball. Used to play basketball with some of my cop buddies in the North Charleston league before I got shot. Those days are over. Can't do much running, but get my exercise with the dogs and try to walk as much as I can. Doctor tells me it's good for my knee. Still get out and do some hunting when I visit my dad at the farm. Decent quail hunting there, plus I try to get out at least once during deer season." Nick padded the Glock under his windbreaker. "Have this one in my apartment but keep the rest of them locked up out at the Academy."

The conversation seemed to be taking the edge off of Allen, and Nick kept it up. "Anyone special in your life?"

"There's a girl in Washington I was seeing before I left. Her name's Heather. We still talk, but it's tough living so far apart. She's with the FBI and works on one of their Evidence Response Teams. There's a lot of field work involved with her job, so she's gone most of the time." Allen was talking about Angela wanting to set him up with one of the nurses when he stopped mid-sentence and grabbed Nick's arm. "There's the truck!" A small delivery truck had just turned into the service road leading to the shipping dock. There was no name printed on the side. It parked to the right of the dock. The driver got out, slid up the back gate of the truck, and removed a dolly. He stacked several cases of soft drinks on the dolly, locked the back gate, and headed up a paved incline to the dock entrance. "That's gotta be our boy," Nick said.

Twenty-five minutes later, the man reappeared. After returning the dolly and half-empty cases to the rear of the truck, he left the shipping area and turned right onto Courtenay. Nick waited until the truck was well over a hundred yards up Courtenay before leaving the parking lot. A light rain began to fall, as the vending truck followed the Crosstown to I-26, eventually exiting in North Charleston at Ashley Phosphate Road. It made three more stops—two auto dealerships and an indoor skating rink. It was approaching 6:00 and the rain was intensifying when the truck drove back up Ashley Phosphate for several miles to a small industrial park. Nick followed the truck into the park, and after a few turns, watched it pull into a small warehouse. The sign on the building read Westcott Distributing, Inc. A large garage door rolled up. The truck drove forward and parked next to a smaller black delivery van.

"What do we do now?" Allen said.

"Note the address and get the license plate numbers of those three cars in front of the building. You got what you needed, now let's get the hell out of here."

Allen quickly recorded the address and plate numbers on his phone, and Nick left the industrial park and headed back toward I-26. It grew even darker, as sheets of rain began moving across the sky tattooing the roof and windshield. A bolt of forked lightning tore across sky followed immediately by the sharp crackle of thunder. Traffic slowed to a crawl. Eyes glued on the road, Nick said, "So, what are you going to do now?"

"Well, unless that vending guy dropped off the drugs at one of his last three stops, now we know where the drugs end up. I need to find out who runs this Westcott company and get a list of their other vending customers. Now that I have a name and address, that shouldn't be a problem."

Nick nodded his agreement. "Right, but think about it. Thompson obviously owed money to Grasso, who we now know runs a loansharking business. Thompson told you it was Grasso, or one of his people, who told him to look the other way when narcotics were delivered to Mercy. There's the link! Grasso and those drugs have got to be part of something much bigger. Listen, Allen, now that you know where the drugs are going, I think it's time to go to the police with what you have."

"Not yet. Anyway, it's not my decision to make. First, I need to find out who's behind Westcott and how big this thing really is. My first priority is getting something solid on the Mercy drug thing. When I think I've got enough to prove what's going on at the hospital, I'll take it all to my employer."

It was clear Nick was less than thrilled with Allen's answer. "I know you've got a job to do, but the longer this thing lasts, the more exposed the rest of us are. Look what happened to Thompson and Davis. Hell, look at your face."

"I know, Nick. But now I've got names. That vending business is part of this Westcott company. Trust me, it won't take me long to get inside Westcott and find out who's behind it and how it's connected to Grasso. Hang in there with me a little longer, I'm almost there."

The rain continued, and it was after 8:00 by the time Nick pulled into the Bee Street garage. When the elevator deposited them on the sixth floor, Allen said, "I'm going into the office in the morning. I should have more information sometime tomorrow. Are you going to be around if we need to get together?"

"Yeah. Josh, Sally, and I take turns taking care of the dogs on the weekends. Josh will be out at the Academy with Zach on Saturday and Sunday, so I'll be around all weekend. Amy and I are going to the aquarium later in the afternoon, but you've got my number. Either way, give me a call and let me know what's going on."

"Will do, and Nick, I really appreciate what you did tonight. I won't forget it."

CHAPTER THIRTY-TWO

IT WAS DARK when Allen awoke Saturday morning. He made himself a cup of coffee and stepped out onto the balcony to watch night evaporate into dawn. The heavy rain from the night before was gone, and he could see a few stars through the clouds. The color was washed out of the night and a subtle gray haze appeared on the horizon—the first hint of approaching dawn. The sky before the sun rose had a calming effect and helped him plan his day.

The swelling in his face was subsiding, and overall, he was feeling much better since the attack. He put on his running shoes and left the building just as a pink slice of sun crested over the horizon. This was his favorite time to run. Allen had several preferred routes throughout the city, and today he headed south past the marina and Coast Guard station toward the Battery, which took him past the thirteen pastel Georgian row houses of Rainbow Row. He continued through the city on his four-mile trek, ending at his Queen Street office.

Allen booted up his computers and mapped out his plan to infiltrate Westcott. The vulnerability of most company's networks never ceased to amaze him. It was like locking the front door of your house but leaving all the windows open.

As expected, Westcott's cybersecurity was sorely lacking, and Allen was able to access files through its website in less than thirty minutes. He'd identified the name of the vending business as Continental Vending, Inc. Once he was in, Allen started downloading Continental Vending's customer list. There were well over a hundred accounts in the greater Charleston area. Mercy General was the only hospital, but there were several urgent care locations and a few of the larger drugstore outlets. These locations were possible targets for the same type of drug theft occurring at Mercy.

It looked as if Westcott was made up of several restaurants, nightclubs, liquor stores, and laundromats. It was a private company, which made tracking down financial data a cumbersome process, but Allen was eventually able to piece together enough information to learn that all these individual operations seemed to be extremely profitable—much more so than would be reasonably expected.

It was clear that all the individual companies operating under the Westcott umbrella were essentially cash businesses. If Westcott was, as he expected, a criminal enterprise, it would be the perfect place to launder money from illicit activities—especially drug trafficking. There was little doubt that Westcott Distributing was a front for a much larger operation, most likely mob-related, like Nick's source at the police department had told him.

It was fairly easy for Allen to identify employees who worked for the various Westcott businesses, but he couldn't find who seemed to be running the company itself. Taxes and other filings for Westcott were made by the Lipton Law Firm located in New Jersey. Corporate filings indicated Westcott was owned by an outfit named Marshall Investments, Inc., and Marshall, in turn, was part of Arcadia Capital, a company headquartered in Cyprus. From there, there were a series of banks and shell companies. Allen had made enough of these offshore searches to know he would eventually find himself staring into a black hole.

He then moved on to identify the owners of the three cars that had been parked in front of the Westcott building. Most people would be surprised at how easy it is to get the names and addresses of car owners by simply having the license plate number. It only took a few minutes for Allen to run the plates. The first was registered to Robert Sanders of 3498 Hartwell Street, Summerville, South Carolina. The owner of the second car, a 2013 Chevrolet Camaro, was registered to an Angelo Vitale of 567 Glenshaw Street, North Charleston. And the third car, a BMW 5 Series, was owned by Max DiMarco of 137 Island Park Drive, Daniel Island, South Carolina.

Allen next ran a rough profile on these individuals, opting to start with DiMarco based solely on the fact that 5 Series go for over $70,000, and his address on Daniel Island was in a very upscale section of the island.

Max DiMarco was born in 1963 in Caldwell, New Jersey. He graduated from Monmouth College with a degree in business and worked in and around New York City for several years until he was convicted of an E felony for falsifying business records. He served a six-month jail term in 2002, but Allen could find no other convictions. He was employed by Prestige Imports based out of New York City for the past twelve years and had lived in the Charleston area for the last three years.

Angelo Vitale had a much more colorful past. He was born in Cleveland, Ohio in 1979. After he graduated high school in 1997, he spent eight years in the Army, serving several tours as an infantryman in Iraq and Afghanistan. He received an honorable discharge in 2006. Since leaving the military, he had a somewhat sketchy employment history and had served time for aggravated assault, robbery, and several lower-level, drug-related offenses. Vitale moved from Cleveland to Charleston in 2014. Allen could find no record of current employment.

Robert Sanders was born in 1992 in Harleyville, South Carolina. He graduated from high school in 2010 and moved to Charleston in 2012, where he worked in the restaurant industry for several years. He had two misdemeanor drug convictions for simple possession—the first for marijuana and the second for cocaine. He received a three-month jail sentence for his second offense and was currently employed as a driver for Continental Vending.

The profiles Allen ran on these guys were fairly simplistic, but it gave him enough to corroborate his supposition that all three were dirty. It seemed reasonable to assume that the kid, Sanders, was a minor player, even though he was involved in transporting the drugs out of Mercy and perhaps other locations on his vending route. Based on his military experience and criminal record, Vitale was probably the operation's muscle. He would be the one to handle any wetwork, if required.

That left DiMarco. He was clearly the boss behind whatever criminal activities were fronted by Westcott. The question was:

Did Allen now have enough to contact Rennells in Chicago? At this point, everything he had was circumstantial. He didn't have security footage actually showing the drugs being taken. He had no direct evidence of Thompson's connection to Russo. He couldn't prove how or who might have poisoned Davis. And even though Westcott appeared shady, he couldn't prove they weren't legitimate, much less a scheme to launder mob money!

Allen was sure he could eventually find a smoking gun somewhere, but time was definitely not on his side. Things were moving too fast. He could probably override whoever was freezing the footage and record the drugs being pilfered, but the next Franklin delivery was almost a week away, and the way things were moving, that seemed like forever.

It was approaching 2:00 when he remembered to call Nick. Nick was on his way to pick up Amy when he answered. "Well, what'd you come up with?"

"A lot," Allen said, "but probably not enough." Allen told him about Continental and the other businesses that were part of Westcott and described Sanders, Vitale, and DiMarco. There was no doubt Westcott was a front for the mob, but he couldn't prove any of it. "We've got nothing solid, and we're running out of time."

"Shit," Nick said, "this whole thing sucks. Listen, there has to be a way to tie all this together. I still say you should go to the cops with what you have. I'm almost at Amy's place. I hate to put this off, but I won't be able to do anything about it today. And, I definitely don't want Amy anywhere near any of this stuff."

"All right," said Allen, "I'll stay on it and call you first thing in the morning. All I need is a little more time. Just watch your back."

CHAPTER THIRTY-THREE

NICK PARKED IN front of Amy's apartment on Folly Road and was walking up to her door, when it opened just enough for him to see that her face and hair were dripping wet. She smiled and said, "Yikes! Nick, I'm really sorry. I was with Cora at the beach all day. Just got out of the shower. Come on in." He followed her in and shut the door behind him. When he turned around, she was standing in front of him, wrapped in nothing but a bath towel. "There's a Coke or beer in the icebox. I'll hurry, I promise." She gave him a quick kiss.

Nick smiled and watched her walk back toward the bathroom, her wet hair falling down her back, the towel not quite big enough to completely cover her tanned and shapely legs. As she disappeared into the steam-filled room, he took a deep breath and whispered to himself, "Jesus."

Amy had John Mayer's Free Fallin' playing quietly in the background. Nick found a Coke in the fridge and sat down at the small kitchen table. Her apartment was smaller than his but tastefully laid out. The walls were a pale blue, and antiqued gray tables accented the lavender sofa and chairs. There were several hanging plants and scented candles throughout the living room and kitchen. The place had a subtle but definitely feminine feel. It was comfortable.

A few minutes later, Nick was standing in front of the refrigerator, a good portion of its door covered with what looked to be family photos. Amy called from her bedroom, "Two more minutes."

He was studying the photos when she joined him in the kitchen. "Thanks for being patient with me."

He slid his arm around her waist and asked, "Are these pictures of your family?"

"Most of them." She pointed at one. "There's my sister, Cora, and my mom. The rest are aunts, uncles, and assorted cousins and some good friends from school."

He pointed to a photo of an older man and said, "Is that your dad?"

She smiled to herself and said, "No. My dad hasn't been in the picture for a long time. I was around six and Cora was four when he left. It's just been the three of us ever since. I do see him occasionally. No hard feelings. We turned out all right, I think."

Nick pulled her close. "I think you turned out just fine. We'd better leave. The aquarium closes at 5:00."

"What a great idea," Amy said. "I can't believe it's been a few years since I've been there."

The Charleston Aquarium is a truly amazing place. Nick purchased an annual pass every year and tried to visit it at least once a month or two. It was home to more than 5,000 animals with a variety of exhibits, Nick's favorite being the two-story, 385,000-gallon tank that was home to Caretta, a 220-pound loggerhead turtle. He liked to finish every one of his visits on the aquarium's huge deck overlooking Charleston Harbor.

They left the aquarium at 5:00, and Nick surprised Amy when they walked down Concord Street and turned into Burwell's Stone Fire Grill. They were seated and both ordered a glass of wine. "Wow, Nick, this is great," Amy said, taking in the atmosphere. "I didn't know we were coming here. I'd have dressed up."

"You look great the way you are. I was debating where to take you tonight, and it came down to Burwell's or The Cup. It was a tough decision, but the steaks are great here, and they have a nice selection of seafood. It's a neat place."

Amy reached across the table and patted his hand. "You made a wise choice." They sat quietly for the next few moments looking over the menu, until she put hers aside and said, "Can I ask you something?"

"Sure, ask away."

"I was working yesterday morning at The Cup, and Allen came in. His face was all bruised and the back of his head was bandaged. I didn't say anything, but he really looked terrible. Do you know what happened?"

Nick had to be careful. "Yeah, apparently he got mugged when he was leaving his office the other night. Actually, he called me after it happened, and I took him to the hospital to get patched up. He'll be fine, says it looks worse than it really is."

"Did they catch whoever did it?"

"No. He told me he didn't see a thing." Nick gave a short laugh. "Says his mom always told him he was 'hard-headed.' Anyway, he's lucky it wasn't worse than it was."

"Wow. That's not like Charleston. Isn't his office right around here?"

"Yeah, it's on Queen."

"Well, it still gives me the shivers."

Their dinners were superb, and when they left the restaurant, they decided to take a leisurely walk up East Bay Street through The French Quarter. Like most nights, downtown Charleston was packed with throngs of people enjoying the theatres, restaurants, and general night life. It was dark by the time they got back to Amy's apartment. When Nick walked her up to the door, she took his hand and led him in. She gave Nick a seductive smile and said, "There's a bottle of wine in the fridge. Why don't you open it? I'm going to change into something more comfortable."

Nick walked to the kitchen and found a bottle of Kendell Jackson Pinot Grigio chilling in the refrigerator and opened it. He returned to the living room with the wine and two glasses. He was admiring a large painting of waves hanging over the sofa when he heard the bedroom door open. Amy appeared wearing a pair of loose-fitting satin pants and a College of Charleston sweatshirt that was cut off midriff. She proceeded to light a few candles and smiled. "A little atmosphere, that's all. Okay with you?"

Nick smiled back. "Sure, atmosphere is a good thing."

They both laughed and Nick poured the wine. He glanced back at the painting and noticed the name scrawled on the lower right corner. "Anderson. Is that Anderson as in Amy Anderson?"

"I wish. My sister painted that. She's amazing." Amy then pointed out two other works by Cora on the far wall. Both were seascapes. "She got all the art genes in the family. She graduated from The Savannah School of Art and Design and teaches art at

Hanahan High School. Some of her pieces are in the Spencer Art Gallery on Broad Street."

Nick sat on the sofa, and Amy joined him. She talked about her relationship with her sister and how important it was to have her support while she was going through her breakup with Paul. "Cora and my Mom are always there for me. Mom's been an elementary school guidance counselor in Mt. Pleasant forever. She's helping out until I graduate and start working. There's no way I can support myself living here and going to school with what I make at The Cup."

Nick nodded in agreement. "Sounds like we both owe a lot to our parents." He raised his wine glass and said, "Here's to your mom and my dad."

Amy tapped her wine glass to his. "I'll drink to that."

They talked for hours about everything from their families to school to what they hoped to do with the rest of their lives. The wine was long gone, and it was approaching 11:00 when Nick finally said, "It's late. I should probably get going."

Amy moved closer to Nick, took his face in her hands, and kissed him. It was a tender kiss, but one filled with promise. Nick slid his hand under her sweatshirt and up the smooth curve of her back. He pulled her close, feeling the softness of her breasts against his chest. She kissed him again, but this kiss was deeper, longer, carrying a sense of urgency. Nick gently lifted her up so that she now straddled him on the sofa. He kissed her neck, breathing in her scent as her hair fell around him. Amy gave out a faint moan and whispered, "Don't go."

Nick hesitated. "Are you sure?"

"Yes, I'm sure." She stood, took his hand, and led him to her bedroom. The candles in the living room eventually flickered out.

CHAPTER THIRTY-FOUR

NICK OPENED HIS eyes and saw a hint of light slipping through the window shades. He glanced at the alarm clock on the nightstand. 6:54. Amy was asleep next to him, her long silky black hair spread out over the pillows, and the gentle curve of her body evident under the white bed sheets. He watched her for several minutes before giving her a soft kiss on her shoulder and whispering, "Good morning, Miss Anderson."

Amy stirred, and without opening her eyes, murmured, "Good morning, Mr. Giordano." She moved closer to him and purred, "What time is it?"

"Almost 7:00. How'd you sleep?"

"Great." She smiled slyly. "But I don't remember either of us actually sleeping much last night."

Nick laughed softly and said, "No, I guess you're right about that. What do you have to do today?"

She sighed. "I work at 11:00. I've also got a paper due next week, so I need to work on that, too. How about you?"

"Allen wants to meet this morning, and then I'll head out to the Academy and work with the dogs. I think I told you Josh will be out there with Zach today. What time do you get off?"

"About 5:00. What does Allen want?"

"I don't know, exactly. I can stop by The Cup after you get off if you want. We can take a walk or something."

Amy smiled. "Or something? No, that'd be nice. I'll get some work done on the paper before I leave this morning." She moved closer to Nick and touched his shoulder, running her hand gently over his gunshot wound. "That's so close to your heart, Nick."

Nick gave her a kiss on the forehead. "Life's a game of inches. I should probably get going."

Amy giggled. "I think I remember you saying that last night."

Nick dressed, and Amy threw on a robe before walking him to her front door. "Thanks for last night. It was wonderful."

Nick pulled her close and said, "I think I'm the one that should be thankful. I'll see you around 5:00."

It was almost 8:00 by the time Nick got back to his apartment. On the way back, he checked his phone and saw Allen had texted him the night before. Nick washed up, changed into a pair of jeans and a work shirt, and grabbed a glass of orange juice before walking down to Allen's condo.

Nick knocked and Allen answered the door, his hair looking like he'd just showered. "Morning, Nick. Come on in. Just got back from a run. Missed you last night."

"Morning, Allen. Yeah, got your text. I was at Amy's." Nick saw several folders and papers spread out on the dining room table.

"I didn't get to spend much time with Amy out at your party, but she seems really nice. She's a pretty girl. How long have you been seeing her?"

"Not long at all, but still long enough for me to want to make sure she doesn't get mixed up in all of this. What did you find out?"

"Well, like I said yesterday, we've got a lot of information about what's going on at Mercy and how it's probably tied to Grasso, Westcott, and DiMarco, but none of it is hard enough to get the police involved."

"I know that," Nick said, obviously frustrated. "The question is: How do we get something solid?"

"Okay, let me finish. If I have to, I can override the freezing of those two cameras in the room where the drug deliveries are made. But I'm not sure we can wait until Friday to do that, and I'm not sure I need to freeze anything. What we need is another good-sized drug delivery from Franklin as soon as possible."

"Yeah, but you just said they're not going to deliver the damn stuff until Friday!"

Allen smiled. "Not unless they get a big rush order for a delivery tomorrow."

Nick shook his head. "I still don't get it."

"I'm going to get into the hospital's computers and send Franklin Pharmaceuticals a narcotics order with instructions it must be delivered tomorrow by 5:00. As soon as I send it, I'll delete it from purchasing's computer. I'll print out new paperwork. But I'll need Angela to make sure the paperwork and note get to the shipping guys, but they can't know it was from her. Whoever's working with them in security, won't know about the order and would have no reason to freeze those cameras. If this works, I'll download the security footage showing the drugs actually being taken and put in the vending machine."

"Sounds like a stretch to me," Nick said. "But even if you can pull it off, we still won't know who's pulling the strings in the security department."

"You're right, but this should be enough for me to get my employer to agree to let us go to the police. I figure if this thing works, the guys in shipping will flip on whoever's calling the shots in security. Then, hopefully, that guy will open the door to what's going on at Westcott. It may be a long shot, but it's the only one I can think of."

"All right," Nick said. "I'll call Angela and make sure she'll be at The Cup in the morning, so I can give her the fake paperwork and note."

Allen thought for a moment. "You know, I'm not sure we should meet at The Cup anymore. Too many eyes and ears. I should have figured that out sooner."

"You're probably right. Go ahead and make that order for the narcotics and print the stuff for Angela. I'll pick it up from you later."

"Sounds good," Allen said. "I'll stop by your place tonight."

"And listen," Nick added, "if this thing doesn't work, I want a promise you'll bring in the cops."

"All right," Allen said. "I'll get ahold of my employer tomorrow morning, tell him what I've got, and insist it's time to bring in the cops no matter what happens. That's a promise."

"Good," Nick said. "And I just thought of something else. Whoever's behind this definitely knows you're a real threat. Who's to say they haven't already bugged your office and phones? You were out cold when that guy attacked you, right?"

Allen thought for a moment. "You may be right." Then he remembered the burner phone Rennells had given him. "I've got another phone I can use."

Nick texted Angela telling her it was important they meet in the morning at Mercy before work, and he'd explain why when they met. He left for the Academy and spend most of the day working with Josh and Zach. He met Amy after work at The Cup, and they had a light meal at Hominy Grill before walking hand in hand to the parking lot for Amy's car. The sun had set, but there was still a peach-colored glow in the western sky. Neither had slept much the night before, and it was catching up with them. It had been a quiet evening, but they were both beginning to realize that they may have found something that had been missing in their lives.

CHAPTER THIRTY-FIVE

ANGEL VITALE AND Anthony Grasso were in Max DiMarco's office at Westcott Distributing Monday morning. Max was not a happy camper. "Anthony, you told me this Thompson guy of yours could be controlled. I trusted your judgment. Then you come to me saying he's becoming somewhat of a—what was it you called him? A liability? So, Angel gets his hands bloody taking care of your liability. Now we got the heat involved. What the fuck?"

Technically, Grasso reported to DiMarco, but he'd been working directly for the bosses in Jersey until they sent in DiMarco three years ago. He didn't like Max, and the feeling was mutual. "Max, let me remind you that it was you who asked me to use Thompson in your little hospital operation. He wasn't a problem until this computer geek, Miller, got involved. I don't give a fuck Angel whacked him. I just don't need a lecture about it."

"Maybe so, but he was still your responsibility," DiMarco replied. "Now, Angel, tell Anthony what else you learned."

"So, there's this problem with Mr. Allen sticking his nose into Mr. DiMarco's hospital business, and I'm supposed to convince him that it's not a healthy thing for him to be doin' what he's doin'. So, I do my thing to convince him, but he don't seem to want to listen. Now, he knows too much, and needs to be dealt with in a more permanent fashion. That's not the problem. The problem is we don't know who else he's told about all Mr. DiMarco's other, shall we say, endeavors. So, Mr. DiMarco would like us to pick up Mr. Allen and find out what he knows before I take care of the permanent part of the solution."

"What do want with me?" Grasso asked DiMarco.

"I want you to go with Angel and help him take care of the problem. I'm sure both of you can be very convincing. Just do it, and don't bother me with the details. That's all. Now go do what you need to do."

CHAPTER THIRTY-SIX

THE NEXT MORNING, Nick was waiting in front of the hospital when Angela arrived. "Well, I'm here. So, what's so important you couldn't tell me over the phone?"

"Sorry, thanks for meeting me. Listen Angela, a lot more has gone down since we saw you on Wednesday."

"I figured that. So, what's up?"

Nick told her that Allen was now pretty sure how the drugs were being stolen. He explained about the vending machine and Allen's meeting with Thompson and his subsequent murder.

"God Nick. I saw that on TV. Just didn't put it together with the hospital stuff."

"Yeah, I know. It's crazy. All right, here's where we are. Allen and I were waiting at the hospital Friday afternoon when the vending guy showed, and we followed him. He ended up at this place way out on Ashley Phosphate called Westcott Distributing."

Nick told her they were pretty sure the drugs from Mercy ended up there and that Westcott is probably nothing more than a front that launders dirty money for some very dirty people. Even though Allen got the names of some of those people, he still didn't have enough solid proof to take to the police.

"We need your help," Nick said.

"I'm listening."

"Okay, the big orders of narcotics come from a company called Franklin Pharmaceuticals, but they usually only deliver to Mercy on Friday afternoons. So, yesterday Allen sent Franklin a bogus order for a lot of pain pills and other narcotics. He made it clear that the stuff needed to be at Mercy by 5:00 today. When it gets to the shipping department, he can download footage from the security cameras there that will show these guys actually stealing the drugs. That's the proof, and it also links the drugs to Westcott."

Angela nodded. "I get all that, but what do you want from me?"

"The guys in shipping replace the actual paperwork that comes with the delivery with fake paperwork, so the missing pills aren't discovered when the pharmacy gets the order." Nick removed an envelope from his pocket. "Here's the fake paperwork."

"You want me to give this to the guys stealing the drugs."

"Exactly," Nick said, "but they can't know it's from you. They've got to assume it's coming from their contact inside Mercy's security department."

Angela thought for a few seconds. "I can do that. There's a young guy in the mailroom. His name is Trevon, and he thinks I'm hot."

Nick smiled, "You are hot, Angela. Zach tells me that several times a day."

"Zach is a smart man," Angela said. "Anyway, I can give this to Trevon and make sure he gets it to whoever without saying where it's from. What's the name of the guy in shipping?"

"There's two," Nick said. "Logan Jefferies and Scott Evans. He can get it to either one. Just let me know when they get it. Remember, they can't know it's from you."

"Okay, I'll do it. But it sure seems like this whole thing is going to blow up no matter what happens this afternoon. I got a bad feeling. If I'm going to do this, Allen's got to promise he'll go to the police even if this thing doesn't work."

"That's what I told Allen last night. He promised me he'd do it."

Angela put the envelope in her purse and said, "All right, but make sure he does it."

CHAPTER THIRTY-SEVEN

THAT MORNING, ALLEN used his burner to call Mr. Rennells on his private line. He answered on the first ring with a simple, "Yes."

"Mr. Rennells, this is Allen Miller. We need to talk."

Allen took the next ten minutes explaining what he'd learned about the narcotics situation at Mercy and how it had expanded into something much more sinister. He then laid out his plan to get the security camera files showing evidence of where and how the drugs were being stolen. "Sir, hopefully this will give you the evidence you need, but whether or not this works, I recommend you go directly to the police. There's already been one person murdered, and others are now at risk."

Rennells' answer came without hesitation. "I agree. The last thing I want is to put you or anyone else in any more danger. I'll call Summerton immediately and tell him to contact the authorities."

"Thank you, sir, but it's important we let that drug delivery go through this afternoon. You need specific evidence, and that will give it to you. Also, I would suggest that you tell only Mr.

Summerton and advise him not to tell anyone else at the hospital, especially Blake Fitzgerald. I'm confident that someone in the hospital's security department is involved. I just don't know who, yet."

"That makes sense," Rennells said. "I'll advise Charles of what's happening and make it clear he's to hold off contacting the authorities until he hears from you. You are to call him as soon as those drugs are delivered this afternoon. Understood?"

"Yes, sir. Consider it done."

"Allen, you've gone above and beyond. We'll talk more when this is over."

Allen then used the burner to call Nick who had just arrived at the Academy. He told him Rennells had agreed to bring in the police as soon as Franklin made their delivery that afternoon. Now it was up to Angela to get those fake documents to shipping. The wheels were beginning to turn.

CHAPTER THIRTY-EIGHT

IT WAS ALMOST 10:00 by the time Allen picked up Sarah and arrived at their Queen Street office. He told her about the fraudulent Franklin order and their need to record what he hoped would be evidence of the theft.

"I talked to Mr. Rennells this morning, and he agrees this whole thing needs to be closed down before someone else gets hurt. Now all we can do is wait and hope everything falls into place. In the meantime, I'd like you to check those camera files again. I also need you to write up a step-by-step explanation of how the narcotics are being stolen—Franklin, the fellows in shipping, the cameras, the vending machine—the whole thing. Summerton will need that along with the security footage when he goes to the police."

"No problem. I just can't believe this will be over today."

"Right. But let's cross our fingers. Remember, it's not what we know, it's what we can prove that will end this thing the right way. Now, I'm going back into Westcott's computer systems to see if I can uncover anything else. I'll pull up the security cameras in shipping in an hour or so, and we can take turns monitoring them."

Thirty minutes later, Allen got a call from Angela. She began telling him she'd given the paperwork to Trevon when Allen stopped her. "Angela, hang up. I'll call you right back." He disconnected and used his burner to call her back. She answered immediately. "Sorry about that," he said. "Go ahead. You were talking about the paperwork."

Angela had given Trevon the envelope, and he promised to deliver it, no questions asked. But there was more. "Listen, when I got to work this morning, there were two detectives in the emergency room. They were talking to Dr. Cramer. He's the doctor that worked on Mr. Davis when they brought him in on Friday. The detectives even asked me a few questions because I was working with Cramer at the time."

"What did they ask you?"

"Just general stuff. Like how well I knew Davis before he got sick, what he was like, did he have any problems, things like that. Do you think it's about the narcotics?"

Allen thought a second. "Maybe. I don't know. They may just be looking into how he got so sick when he was working there. Keep your eyes open, and let me know if you learn anything else. Thanks again for doing this, Angela."

It was noon when Allen gave up on Westcott and turned his attention to the security footage. In addition to the two cameras in the narcotics room, he now had accessed an exterior camera showing the entire shipping dock area. Nothing to do now but watch and wait.

~~~~
~~~~

Nick spent the balance of the morning and early afternoon working the dogs with Josh and Zach, the events unfolding at Mercy dominating his thoughts.

CHAPTER THIRTY-NINE

BY 2:00, SARAH had finished her written analysis and joined
Allen in his office. The next hour passed slowly as they both
stared at the computer monitors, their silence broken only by brief
comments or questions of what was to come. The security
cameras in the drug-checking room activated several times when
employees got drinks from the vending machine. Finally, at 3:25,
Sarah sat bolt upright and said, "Allen, the truck!"

There it was. The Franklin Pharmaceutical truck was backing
up to the dock. Both were out of their seats staring at the monitor.
The driver exited, unlocked and raised the truck's rear gate, and
began to load three bins onto a dolly. He then lowered and locked
the gate before disappearing from the monitor recording the dock
area. Several tense minutes followed before the two narcotic room
cameras activated, showing Jefferies and Evans entering with the
bins.

Evans cut the colored ties. Allen smiled as Jefferies, glanced
at one of the cameras, and scratched the back of his head. Both
men left the room for about five seconds before returning and

removing the top of the three bins, now assuming they were no longer being recorded. Evans pulled out what must have been the forged paperwork from under his shirt and studied it for a minute. After speaking briefly to his partner, he began removing several bottles and boxes from each bin. Meanwhile, Jefferies had opened the locked side panel on the vending machine and began transferring the bottles and boxes into the open compartment.

Allen whispered, "Jesus Christ, Sarah. It's happening."

The whole transfer took less than four minutes. Jeffries locked the side compartment, and Evans replaced the actual paperwork with Allen's fabricated document. He quickly put the tops back on the bins. Both men left the room for about four or five seconds before returning and going through their normal process of inventorying the contents of the bins. Twenty-five minutes later, both Jefferies and Evans signed the inventory document, resealed the bins, and removed them from the room.

Both Allen and Sarah were quiet, both trying to mentally digest what they'd just witnessed. Suddenly, Allen fell back into his white leather chair and said, "Got 'em!"

Sarah was beaming. "Allen, you did it!"

"No, Sarah, we did it!" He looked at his watch. "All right, I need to call Mr. Summerton. But, first, we've got to assume we weren't the only ones watching those security cameras. There's a chance whoever's monitoring the hospital's cameras also saw it and was sharp enough to figure out what was really going on. If that happened, we also have to assume that whoever's involved in the security department will eventually know their cover was blown. I'll call Summerton and then make copies of all three camera files. I've also got to call Nick to let him know what we've got. Jesus, I still can't believe it."

Allen made the call to V.P. Summerton. Mr. Rennells had already brought him up to speed on the situation, and he was expecting Allen's call. Allen told him they now had irrefutable evidence of the crime in the form of security camera files.

"I'm astounded," Summerton said. "No way would I have thought something like this could ever happen at my hospital. I know Police Chief Taylor. I'll tell him what we know, and he'll know how to proceed. I'd like you to bring those camera files to police headquarters as soon as possible."

"No problem, and I'd like to bring my assistant with me. She's been deeply involved in the entire investigation."

"That's fine, bring whoever and whatever you think will help. I'll contact you should things change."

Allen gave Summerton the number of his burner and joined Sarah, who was making additional copies of her write-up. "I just talked to Mr. Summerton, and he wants me to meet him at the police station on Lockwood. I told him I was bringing you with me."

"I'd have been pissed if you didn't."

"Good. You better call Dave and let him know this will probably be a late night for you." He returned to his office, called Nick, and let him know the drug delivery had arrived at Mercy and that the entire theft was now recorded. "Mr. Summerton, the V.P. at Mercy, is going to call the chief of police. He wants me and Sarah at the station. I'll make sure he knows about Westcott."

"Great, Allen. Do you think I need to be there?"

"No. But eventually they're going to want to talk to both you and Angela. For now, just relax and know it won't be long before this whole thing is over and done with."

"Yeah, man, and not soon enough, as far as I'm concerned. Really, Allen, this is great news. Keep me in the loop."

"Definitely. I'll call you later, and thanks for all your help."

Allen knew they would probably be at the police station a long time and should eat something before they left. It was after 5:00 when he called Blossom's, a restaurant right around the corner on East Bay, and ordered sandwiches and drinks. He told Sarah the food would be ready in about twenty minutes, gave her a fifty, and asked her to pick it up. She left for the restaurant about ten minutes later.

~~~~

Angel Vitale had been in the lobby of the Vendue Hotel across the street watching Allen's office for the past hour. As soon as he saw Sarah leaving, he called Grasso who was waiting a block up Queen in a black Ford van driven by one of his men. A minute later, the van was in front of Allen's office, and Grasso was heading up the stairs with Angel right behind him.

Allen had just finished making multiple flash drive copies of the security camera's digital files when he heard the door to the outer office open. "That was quick!" he called out, thinking Sarah was already back with the food. He waited for her response, and hearing none, got up and headed for his office door. As soon as he reached it, something large plowed into him. The air was pulled out of his chest as he was sent sprawling to the floor.

Grasso shoved his forearm into Allen's face and held him down. For the second time in the past week, Angel Vitale plunged a hypodermic needle into Allen's neck, injecting him with another batch of thiamylal sodium. Allen fought back hard trying to get
~~~~

out from underneath Grasso, but he was no match. In about twenty seconds, he began to lose consciousness. Fifteen seconds later, he was out cold.

Angel saw the flash drives on Allen's desk, grabbed them, and stuffed them in his pants pocket. He was tempted to smash the computer monitors again but quickly realized it would be better to leave the office untouched. That way, no one would know they'd been there. Angel was by Allen's desk looking for anything else he might take with him, when he heard Grasso call out, "Vitale, give me a hand out here!"

Grasso had dragged Allen's body to the top of the stairs, but that was as far as he could go on his own. Allen was only about 170 pounds, but in his condition, he was dead weight and not easy to lift.

Together, they managed to get Allen down the stairs. Angel stepped through the door and checked to make sure no one was watching and then helped Grasso carry Allen out and into the waiting black van. Just as they were hoisting him into the back, Sarah rounded the corner onto Queen and saw what was happening. She froze for a few seconds, then dropped the bag of food and started running toward the van. But by the time she got there, it was already half way up Queen toward Meeting Street. Seconds later, it made a hard right onto Meeting and disappeared.

Sarah was stunned and just stood there staring up an empty Queen Street, her heart pounding. She quickly snapped out of it and raced up the stairs to the office. She had no idea what to do or who to call. She shut her eyes, trying to calm herself and then grabbed her cell phone. She scrolled until she found the name Giordano then punched the number so hard she almost dropped the phone.

"Low Country Police Dog Academy." It was Sally.

Sarah, still trying to catch her breath, yelled, "Giordano, I need to talk to Giordano."

"Who's calling, please?"

"Allen Miller," Sarah blurted. "I mean my name is Sarah, and I work for Allen Miller. It's important!"

"Hold the line, please," Sally said, calmly. She put the call on hold, and walked to Nick's office. "Nick, you've got a call. It's from a lady that says she works for your friend, Allen Miller. She sounds upset."

Nick was in his office with Josh and Zach reviewing the progress of the individual dogs. "All right, Sally, I'll get it." He picked up the phone, "Nick Giordano."

Sarah had managed to calm herself a bit. "Mr. Giordano, my name is Sarah Pryor, and I work for Allen Miller. Allen told me you know about the drugs being taken from Mercy General. He told me to call you if anything bad happened." Sarah was crying now. "They took him. Someone's kidnapped Allen!"

"Okay, Sarah. Take a breath. Try to calm down. Now, tell me what happened."

Sarah told him she saw two men throw Allen into the back of a black van outside their office. The moment Nick heard "black van," he knew exactly who'd kidnapped Allen. He and Allen had spotted a black van in the Westcott warehouse. "Okay, Sarah. Where are you now?"

"Downtown in our office."

"Sarah, are you married?"

"Yes."

"Okay, Good. You need to get ahold of your husband. Tell him there's been an accident, and he needs to pick you up right away."

"He works at the college. We live right there. It's faster if I walk home and meet him there."

"Good, Sarah. Then you need to do that. Stay put when you get home, and I'll call you as soon as I know anything. You did good."

"Okay, I'm leaving now. Please, call me."

"I will. I promise. Now go."

Josh and Zach had caught only half of the conversation, but enough to realize something bad had happened to Allen.

"Shit, Nick," Josh said. "What is it?"

Nick was up and out of his seat, now in full cop mode. "That was Allen's assistant. She said he's been kidnapped. I know there's a lot you two don't know, but I'll explain it all later. Josh, do you have your gun with you?"

"Locked in my truck. Beretta M9. What is it?"

Nick ignored Josh's question and asked Zach if he was carrying.

"No, don't own one anymore."

Nick turned, pulling his keys from his pocket, and walked directly to a locker in the rear corner of his office. He unlocked the padlock and swung open the door. He pulled out a Benelli M2 Field 12 Gauge shotgun and a box of Fiocchi High Velocity shells. "Zach, take these." He then removed his Browning Bolt-Action rifle. "Josh, go to the kennels and get Ringo. We'll meet you at your truck."

Josh had been in enough firefights to know what was coming. He turned and headed toward the kennels without hesitation. Sally caught her breath when she saw Zach and Nick leaving his office carrying guns.

"Nick, what—"

Before she could get another word out, Nick said, "Sally, Isaiah's in the back cleaning the new kennels. I need you to get him, lock up, and go home. I'll explain later." He was past her and at the door when he turned, gave her a reassuring smile, and said, "Please, just do it."

Zach and Nick were waiting at Josh's Dodge Ram. Nick was about to call Steve Williams to let him know what was happening but was interrupted when Josh returned from the kennels with Ringo, a ninety-pound male shepherd who'd just completed his training. Zach opened the back door, and Ringo jumped in. Zach followed, slamming the door shut behind him. Nick was already in the front seat when Josh slid in. "Where to?"

Nick stared straight ahead and said, "Take Main to 17. Move it!"

Josh swung the Dodge out of the parking lot and punched it, cinder stone flying from under the tires. Nick looked at his watch. Almost 6:00. Rush hour traffic would still be bad on I-26. "Josh, we're going to Ashley Phosphate Road out past the airport, but the traffic on 26 will be a bitch. Take Bees Ferry to 61."

"Got it," Josh answered. "What are we walking into?"

"The two guys who grabbed Allen put him in the back of a black van. Allen and I saw what must have been that same van out at an industrial park off Ashley Phosphate Road the other night. That's got to be where they're taking him."

"Who are these guys, and why'd they snatch Allen?" Josh asked.

"Allen was doing some confidential computer security work," Nick said, "and stumbled on a major criminal operation. Drugs, gambling, and a bunch of other shit all connected to some syndicate out of New Jersey. I don't know anything more about these guys, but we've got to figure they've got guns and know how to use them."

Nick was in the middle of explaining how they'd followed the vending truck to the Westcott building when he stopped, slammed his fist into the dashboard, and said, "Shit!" Everything had happened so fast, he'd completely forgotten to call Steve Williams. He pulled out his cell and called Steve, hoping he'd still be in his office.

The phone rang several times before he answered. "K-9, Williams."

"Steve, thank God you're still there!"

"Allen? I was just leaving, What's the matter?"

"Listen. I need your help. Remember when I asked you about that Grasso guy? I can't go into all of it now, but there's been a kidnapping. I need you to call the North Charleston station and get them out to…damn it, I can't remember the address. It's a warehouse in one of those industrial parks out past the Air Force Base off Ashley Phosphate. I think it was Fisher Road. The name of the company is Westcott Distributing. They can look it up."

"Okay, Westcott Distributing. Got it. Where are you?"

"We're on the way there. Josh and Zach are with me."

"All right, I'll call North Charleston and have them send out a team. Nick, listen to me. Don't do anything until they get there!"

"Just get them out there, Steve!"

Josh turned and looked straight at Nick. "How the hell did you get wrapped up in this?"

"Okay, it's a long story, and there's no time to explain everything. But you need to know that Allen is more than just some computer guy. He used to work for the government doing highly classified cybersecurity work for Homeland Security. Narcotics were being stolen from Mercy General Hospital, and his company was secretly hired to investigate. That's when we discovered the connection to the syndicate in Jersey."

Zach had not said a word up to this point, but straightened up when he heard the words Mercy General. He leaned forward, "Does Angela know about this?"

"She does, Zach," replied Nick, "but don't worry, she's totally safe."

They had just passed the Air Force Base and were still about five minutes from the industrial park. The sky had darkened, and the smell of rain was in the air. Land away from the coast absorbs heat from the intense sun, and the rising air draws moisture in from the ocean. This results in towering thunderclouds and heavy late-afternoon downpours. Nick thought the dark clouds were a harbinger of what was about to happen.

Bands of rain were a few miles off as Josh turned right onto Ashley Phosphate Road. Nick pointed ahead and said, "Turn right up ahead at the next light." A few more turns. Nick saw the Westcott building. "Josh, pull past it and park in the next lot."

Josh swung the truck into an empty lot about a hundred feet or so from the side of the Westcott building. There were four cars parked in front, along with the Continental delivery truck. Nick immediately recognized the BMW and Camaro he'd seen in front of the warehouse on Friday.

"You guys stay here," Nick said. "I'll go around to the side of the warehouse where the garage is and see if that van's in there."

Nick opened the door, but Josh grabbed his arm. "You're not going anywhere. You can't move fast enough with that leg of yours. I'll recon the place." It was clear there'd be no further discussion. Josh left the truck, ran across the lawn toward the warehouse, and disappeared behind the rear of the building just as the first drops of rain began to fall.

Several minutes passed before Josh returned, his tee shirt and pants soaked from the sheets of rain now coming down. He slammed the door shut and said, "The van's in there and so is Allen. I saw four dudes. They're in the garage and they've got him tied to a chair. Looks like they've already worked him over pretty good."

"Shit. Any weapons?" Nick asked.

"Saw one guy with a sawed off, but I'm sure there's more."

Nick knew he should wait for the cops, but he didn't know how much longer Allen would last. There was no way they'd let him out of this thing alive. But Nick couldn't forget the decision he'd made seven years earlier and the lives it had cost. "Ah, fuck it," he finally said. "Zach, give me the rifle."

The three of them left the truck. Josh attached a control leash to Ringo and started across the lawn, now covered with puddles. Nick followed with his Browning and Zach was right behind him, both hands gripping the shotgun.

CHAPTER FORTY

MAX DIMARCO WAS in the garage with Anthony Grasso and his driver, Chico. Vitale had just finished another round with his blackjack on Allen, this time concentrating on his knees and ankles. "Ease up, Angel," DiMarco said. "I want him alive until we find out just how much he knows and who else he's told. I'm shutting down the hospital thing, but Jersey wants to know how deep this guy's into our operation."

"I know what I'm doing," Angel said with a twisted smile.

Allen sat motionless, his hands fixed behind him and his ankles secured with thick plastic ties. His face was a mess. His head had slumped forward. Blood dripped from his nose and mouth. The front of his shirt was soaked dark red with blood. The stitches around his mouth had been torn open.

Angel, wearing black leather gloves, bent down in front of Allen and lifted his head. "Come on, Allen. I really don't want to do this anymore. Just answer a few questions, and you walk out of here. I'm a reasonable guy. Who you workin' for?"

Allen said nothing.

Angel moved closer. "Who else knows about the hospital?"

Allen opened his eyes, almost swollen shut from the beating, and muttered something.

"What was that, my friend?"

"Fuck you."

Angel raised up, letting Allen's face fall back to his chest. "Geeze, Allen," he said. "That wasn't very nice." Angel walked over to a workbench and took a minute surveying the tools hanging from the Masonite pegboard and metal shelves above it. He removed a pair of six-inch needle nose pliers and returned to Allen. He read the brand name on the pliers and said, "Stanley; they make good tools, you know?" He walked around the back of the chair and put Allen's pinky finger between the teeth of the pliers. "One more time, Allen. Who else knows about Mercy?"

Allen said nothing.

Angel gripped the pliers tighter and started to squeeze and twist until he heard a snap. Allen screamed and then slumped. He'd passed out.

"That's enough!" DiMarco said. "I don't think he knows much, or he'd have already told us. Go ahead and get rid of him, but not here. Take him somewhere else and make sure the body disappears this time."

Angel nodded. "What about his secretary? There's also the nurse and the other guy."

"No, not yet," said DiMarco. "I need to talk to my people first."

"Yes, sir. You're the boss. Chico, get this asshole in the van."

Vitale used the pliers to cut the plastic tie around Allen's wrists and ankles. Chico opened the rear doors of the black van and was about to retrieve Allen when there was a sharp crack. He jerked back a step. He looked confused for an instant then looked down at his chest. A small spot of red appeared. His legs buckled, and he collapsed to the concrete floor. The rifle shot had come from the far end of the garage. Both Vitale and Grasso dove behind the van and pulled their guns. DiMarco ducked and ran back through the door leading to the building's office. Angel and Grasso scrambled to their knees, pressing themselves tight against the van.

"What the fuck?" Grasso growled.

Neither man moved. The garage was now quiet except for the pounding of rain on the metal roof. Angel inched his way to the rear of the van and peered around the back fender toward where the shot had come from. Industrial fluorescent ceiling lights illuminated the entire area. Angel could clearly see the door at the far end of the building was open. Then a hand reached around the corner of the door and pressed a large red button on the wall.

A metal encased light next to the door began to flash red followed by the sound of the metal pulley engaging.

Grasso rolled away from the van and fired four rounds from his 357 Magnum toward the far door. The boom of the shots echoed through the room, as the heavy steel garage door began to slowly open, allowing a gust of wind and wall of rain to sweep in under it. Grasso was able to retreat behind the van just in time to hear the thud of two bullets strike it. A third round shattered the side window, showering him with shards of glass. He made a snap decision and ran toward the opening garage door firing two more rounds at the far door. The garage door was half way up when he reached it. He was almost outside when the explosion from the shotgun blast lifted him off the ground. Zach racked another round and was moving to his left out of the line of fire when

Angel shot him. The slug grazed Zach's forearm and the shotgun fell harmlessly to the ground.

Angel made a run for it. He was through the garage door and almost to his Camaro when he caught sight of the dog. He had his revolver leveled when Ringo was airborne. Before he could pull the trigger, Ringo slammed into Angel's chest, sending him and his gun flying over the hood of the Camaro. He had no chance. When Angel realized what had happened, Ringo had him by the back of his leg and was dragging him across the parking lot.

By this time, DiMarco had made it to his office, removed his S&W revolver from his desk drawer, and slipped out the front door. He could hear sirens and see the blue and red lights of police cars in the distance. He'd just pulled open the door to his BMW when he heard a voice behind him. "I wouldn't do that if I were you."

He whirled around and saw the rifle pointing at his chest. "Nice and easy," Nick said, "Put the gun on the ground."

Max smiled. "Okay, you got me. Just don't shoot. How the hell did you know?"

"Put the gun down, now!" Nick repeated, this time louder.

The two men locked eyes. It was clear Max had other ideas. In one quick motion, he raised his revolver, but never got off the shot. The bullet hit his shoulder, spinning him around, the gun falling next to him as he slid down the side of the Beamer. Nick walked up to him and kicked the gun away.

DiMarco was on the ground, his teeth clenched in pain. Nick stood over him and grinned. "This is for my friend, Allen." He spun the rifle around like a baton, raised it high in the air, and brought the butt of his Browning down squarely on the top of DiMarco's head.

He retrieved DiMarco's gun, walked into the parking lot, and laid the revolver and his Browning on the ground in front of him. Then he raised both hands high above his head. Three North Charleston squad cars roared into the parking lot. One of them skidded to a stop in front of Nick. The officers were out of their car seconds later, pointing their guns at him. He slowly dropped to his knees, laid face down on the ground, and extended both hands behind his back.

The rain had slackened but still was falling when he felt the handcuffs snap around his wrists. Then he heard someone say, "Ah Christ, Giordano. I told you not to do anything until we got here! Uncuff him."

The handcuffs were removed. Nick rolled over and saw Steve Williams staring down at him. Steve grabbed his hand and pulled him up. He glared at Nick, shook his head, and said, "You got some explaining to do, son! What the hell happened?"

"Four total, three down, two probably dead," Nick said. He pointed at DiMarco. "This one's alive. Josh, Zach, and one of my dogs are around here somewhere. Guy named Allen Miller is in the garage. He's on our side, and he's been beat up bad. Someone needs to get him to the hospital."

Williams told one of the officers to collect the guns and take care of DiMarco. He told another one to request more units, along with the EMTs, and to check on the man in the garage. He then glanced at the two other squad cars. "Nick, come with me."

The four officers had Zach and Josh on their knees with their hands behind their backs. They'd retrieved the 12 Gauge and Josh's Beretta, and kept their distance as Ringo stood beside Josh panting and watching Angel Vitale intently. Vitale was on the ground holding what was left of his right calf. Most of the lower pant leg had been torn away, exposing the gruesome evidence of Ringo's attack. The situation remained tense until Williams told the officers to stand down. Josh looked at Nick, nodded toward the garage, and said, "Allen's inside."

Williams ordered the officers to secure the area and waved Nick to follow him in. Allen had crawled to the corner of the garage and was sitting with his back against the workbench, legs sprawled out in front of him, his head slumped against his chest. His face was bleeding profusely, his left eye nearly swollen shut.

"Jesus!" Williams said.

Allen heard Williams and lifted his head slightly. Nick knelt next to him and said, "It's okay, now. We've got you."

A minute later, an officer joined them and confirmed they'd secured the area and found the bodies of two white males, both deceased.

Nick knew additional police units would be on the way, and as soon as the detectives arrived, the whole crime scene would be locked down tighter than a cat's ass. He also knew he'd be separated from Josh and Zach—the three of them would all be interrogated individually. It would be a long night. Nick looked at Williams and said, "Steve, I need to make a quick call before this thing gets shut down."

Steve knew he should refuse, but he went ahead. "Just make it quick. Listen to me this time, please."

"Thanks, Steve." He pulled out his cell and called Sally Reed. She answered immediately. "Sally, everyone's okay. Don't worry. I can't talk now, but I'll explain everything tomorrow."

"Thank God, Nick. Isaiah's here with me. What happened?"

"Sally, I've got to go. We're all fine. I'll explain tomorrow." He hung up before she could say another word. Then he called Amy.

"Listen, Amy. I only have a minute here. There's been…a situation, but everyone's okay. Josh and Zach are with me. Nobody's hurt. I can't explain now, but I need you to call Angela. Tell her Zach is with me, and he's fine." He could hear more sirens approaching.

"Angela's here with me now. Oh, my God, Nick, what happened?"

"Amy, I've got to go. Don't worry. I'll call you as soon as I can!"

Nick hung up, and Steve held out his hand. "Nick, that's enough. Give me the phone."

"One more, Steve." He found Sarah Pryor's number in his contacts and called her. He told her Allen was hurt but would be okay, and that he'd probably be taken to MUSC emergency. She could check there. He hung up and gave Steve the phone. "Hang onto this until they're done with me. All right?"

"Now, I need you, Josh, and Zach against that back wall, but separated. No guns, no phones. And make sure your damn dog is collared and under control. The shit is going to hit the fan any minute now!"

Nick remembered Allen was supposed to meet Charleston's Police Chief and told Steve. "I'll take care of that, Nick. Now, go get your dog."

The "shit" arrived, and the fans were on full blast when three more North Charleston police cars roared into the parking lot. Officers had the whole area cordoned off with yellow crime scene tape when the detectives and EMTs arrived ten minutes later.

Steve recognized the two homicide detectives and gave them a quick recap of what he knew. It was another half an hour before Charleston County's CSI team arrived. Zach's arm was treated and bandaged, and Allen was taken to MUSC. The forensic technicians began their job of collecting and cataloging evidence that would later be analyzed in the lab.

Both DiMarco and Vitale had been treated for their injuries and carted off in handcuffs. Grasso and Chico had been put in body bags and were on their way to the Medical Examiner's Office at the county morgue.

It was well past 9:00 by the time CSI technicians had completed their work, and the detectives had finished interviewing Nick, Josh, and Zach. When they were finally cut loose, Nick retrieved his phone from Steve and saw there had been ten missed calls from Amy and Angela. He called Amy.

"Oh, my God, Nick. Are you okay?"

"I'm all right, Amy. Where are you now?"

"I'm at my place. Angela's still with me."

"Listen, stay there. The police are letting us go now. Zach and I will be there in about half an hour. Everything's okay. We'll tell you what happened as soon as we get there."

Josh had Ringo in the back of his truck when Nick and Zach joined him. "Josh, drop me and Zach off at Amy's place on Folly Road and then take Ringo back to the Academy. Okay?"

"Right. Jesus, Nick, I still can't believe you got mixed up with the mob."

"There's more to it but not tonight, Josh."

"Yeah, well, you know what they say, 'You sleep with dogs, you wake up with fleas.'"

Nick turned and looked at Ringo in the back seat. He smiled and said, "Watch your language."

Josh returned the smile. "Right, bad analogy, but you know what I mean." The rain had stopped as they took the ramp onto I-26 and headed to Amy's apartment on James Island.

CHAPTER FORTY-ONE

AMY WAS WAITING outside with Angela when Josh pulled up in front of her apartment. She was in Nick's arms the moment he stepped out of the truck. "We were so worried. Zach was supposed to pick up Angela at the hospital after work, but he never showed. She kept calling him, but he didn't answer, so she got ahold of me, and I picked her up. God, we didn't know what to think!"

"I'm sorry, but everything was happening all at once. Let's all go inside, and I can explain."

Angela had her arm around Zach, a look of concern on her face when she saw his bandaged arm.

Before heading to her apartment, Nick broke their embrace, and said, "Amy, give me a minute, okay?" He returned to the truck and leaned in the passenger-side window. "Josh, our trucks are still out at the Academy. Zach and I'll probably spend the night here, and Amy will drop us off out there in the morning." He paused for a moment before continuing. "Josh, I don't know what to say. I had no idea all this shit was going to go down the way it did.

You guys were amazing out there tonight. There's no way I can thank you enough."

"Listen, buddy, you've always been there for me when I needed help. No need to say another word." He smiled. "Anyway, I think we did all right for an old gimpy ex-cop and two broken down Army grunts."

"Yeah, I guess you're right, but don't forget Ringo. Did you see the number he did on that guy's leg?" Nick leaned back out of the window, patted the roof of the truck, and said, "Now, get out of here, and we'll see you tomorrow." All four of them stood arm in arm and watched Josh drive away.

Once inside, Angela noticed blood had begun to seep through Zach's bandage, so she took him into the bathroom to change the dressing.

Amy asked Nick if he wanted something to drink.

"A beer sounds good, if you've got one," he said.

"Definitely, and Angela and I'll join you. Got some ginger ale for Zach. Angela and I made some sandwiches. We figured you two probably didn't have anything to eat."

"Great. Food's been the last thing on my mind, but you're right, I'm starving." Amy and Nick brought the food and drinks out to the living room, and a few minutes later, they were joined by Angela and Zach.

"Nick," Angela said. "I haven't told Amy anything, and you definitely owe her an explanation. She doesn't know what's been going on at the hospital, with Thompson, Davis, or this thing with Westcott. Plus, I want to know if you recorded the camera files on those guys in shipping this afternoon. Now, start talkin' and don't leave anything out."

You can imagine the look on Amy's face. She was clearly overwhelmed. "All right, Angela. I'll start at the beginning. It all started when Allen got hired to…"

And so, Nick went on to explain everything that had happened over the past several weeks and their possible future ramifications. The narrative took almost an hour, and it was past 11:00 by the time he finished.

Everyone was physically and mentally drained and ready to crash. Amy got blankets and pillows for Angela and Zach who bedded down in the living room, while she and Nick retired to her bedroom.

As soon as Nick closed the bedroom door, he said, "Let's plan on getting up early to go see how Allen's doing. I'm sure they kept him overnight at MUSC. He was busted up pretty bad. I don't know if you have to work or have class, but could you drop us off at the Academy after we see Allen?"

"Sure, I already called work and told them I need the day off, and I only have one class. I can cut that one."

"Thanks." He pulled Amy close. "I can't remember, did I ever tell you how great you are?"

Amy smiled. "I seemed to remember the other night when you mentioned that several times, but feel free to tell me again."

"Amy, I think you're great."

"Thank you, Mr. Giordano, now prove it."

CHAPTER FORTY-TWO

ANGELA AND ZACH were up having coffee when Amy and Nick joined them in the kitchen. "Good morning, guys," Nick said. "How's that arm, Zach?"

"Fine, just a scratch," Zach mumbled.

"Fine, my ass," Angela said. "That's no scratch. You were moaning last night, and you're seeing a doctor as soon as we get to the hospital this morning."

Nick laughed. "Moaning, Zach?"

"Hush, Nick," Amy said. "Angela's right, someone needs to check that arm."

"I need to call Allen's assistant to see if she has any updates on Allen. She should know the latest."

Sarah answered and told him she was waiting at MUSC when the EMTs brought Allen in and stayed there for several hours.

"He's doing surprisingly well considering what he went through," Sarah said. "I talked with the doctors last night. They said he has a few broken ribs, a broken finger, and some bad cuts and bruises on his face and legs, but no serious internal injuries. I was able to see him for a few minutes before I left. He doesn't remember much of anything after he was attacked in our office."

"Thanks, Sarah. That's all good news. We're going over to the hospital in a while to see him."

"You'd better call ahead. His parents were there last night and got me in. They're only letting family in to see him, and visiting hours aren't until 9:00."

"Thanks, again. We'll do that." Nick hung up and passed on the information about Allen's condition to Zach and the girls. "I'll see if I can get through to Allen's room. We can't get in to see him until 9:00, so let's grab some breakfast at Halo's. That's right next to the hospital."

They all piled in Amy's 2012 VW. They had a quick breakfast and were at the hospital's reception desk by 8:45. The receptionist checked to make sure their names were on the visitors' list and directed them to the elevator. When they arrived at the fourth floor, they checked in at the nursing station and were told visitations were limited to no more than five minutes.

Allen's room was dark when they entered. His face and head were heavily bandaged and his right hand was in a cast. Nick smiled down at him. "You look like shit, Allen."

Allen winced when he smiled. "Feels like I went ten rounds with Rocky Balboa. Jesus, I spent all those years dealing with really bad dudes at CERT without so much as a scratch—now look at me. What the hell happened last night?"

"We've only got a few minutes," Nick said. "All you need to know now is that they got the bad guys. I'll tell you the whole story when you get out of here. The doctor said you need to rest. Can we do anything for you?"

"Thanks, Nick. My mom and dad just left. I'm good."

Just then, there was a soft knock at the door. Nick turned and saw two men in suits—the detectives who interviewed them at the Westcott the night before. He turned back to Allen. "We'll check on you later. No more fistfights. All right?" Angela and Amy touched Allen's arm and walked to the door. The detectives nodded to Nick and Zach as they left the room.

After leaving MUSC, they made the short walk down the street to Mercy General, where Angela dragged Zach into the emergency room and had one of the doctors check his arm. The EMTs had only cleaned and closed the wound with butterfly bandages the night before. After examining the wound, the emergency room doctor stitched up Zach's arm and put a new dressing on it. Angela had everyone out of the emergency room in less than an hour.

When Amy, Nick, and Zach arrived at the Academy, Josh was already in the office with Sally and Isaiah. Amy didn't have to work, so she stayed awhile. Josh had given Sally and Isaiah a brief explanation of what had happened the night before, but they were anxious to hear more from Nick and Zach. Of course, Zach had little to say, but Nick gave them his account and answered all their questions. They talked for almost an hour until Nick broke it up and said they needed to put in some work with the dogs. He was leaving the office when he noticed Isaiah frowning at him.

"You okay, Isaiah?"

"No, sir."

"What's up?"

Isaiah shook his head. "The three of ya' left old Isaiah here when y'all went to help that Allen fella yesterday. Ya' shoulda' took me, I coulda' helped."

Nick put his hand on his shoulder and said, "Of course you could have, but I needed someone to stay back and take care of Miss Sally. But listen here. Every time it got hairy with those crooks last night, I just asked myself, 'What would Isaiah do?'"

"Yeah," Isaiah said, the frown easing a bit, "but ya' still coulda' used my help."

"You're right. Now, it's feeding time. You got some dogs that need your help."

"I'm on it, Boss."

Nick walked Amy to her car and asked, "See you later?"

"Absolutely. What do you want to do?"

"I don't know. I've had enough excitement for a while. How about someplace quiet?"

"How about you come on over to my place after work. It's quiet." She winked, gave him a peck on the cheek, and whispered, "But I can't promise there won't be a little excitement waiting for you."

CHAPTER FORTY-THREE

THE SHOOTING AT Westcott hit the press the following day and the coverage stayed waist-deep in the papers and on the internet for several days as more information came to light. FBI and DEA agents quickly took over the main investigation as it related to DiMarco, Westcott, and their suspected connection to mob activities in New Jersey. It took a while, but after several days of interrogation and threats of dropping RICO charges on them, both DiMarco and Vitale agreed to a deal and flipped on their connection to the boys in Jersey. Vitale refused to admit his involvement in Chuck Thompson's murder, but prosecutors were confident they would eventually be able to tag him with the crime. Both men were sent to the Federal Correctional Institute in Estill, South Carolina while they awaited their formal testimony and sentencing.

While much of the traditional Mafia and La Cosa Nostra crime families have been replaced by other criminal elements, one long-standing rule has survived—you snitch, you die. It took only two weeks at the Estell facility before Max DiMarco was found dead in a shower room, his throat slit ear to ear. Angel Vitale was immediately transferred to solitary confinement. The move was not only for his own protection, but, more importantly, to make sure he could testify if and when federal charges were filed. DiMarco's murder made Vitale all the more important—the Feds were after the head of the snake.

Robert Sanders, the Continental Vending driver, confessed to his part in the theft of the narcotics, but knew little of the inner workings of Westcott's larger operations. He also gave the authorities the names of three other pharmacies involved in the vending machine caper. He pled guilty to grand larceny and was sentenced to a fine of $15,000 and a six-year term in the state penitentiary in Columbia.

Logan Jefferies and Scott Evans were having a beer at Moe's Crosstown Tavern in celebration of another successful "vending machine drug heist" when four Charleston City police officers entered the bar. Handcuffed, scared, and confused, Jefferies and Evans were taken to the station for questioning. They were put in separate rooms and left to fret for an hour before detectives questioned them. It took only a few minutes for both to roll over on their contact in the hospital's security department.

Three hours later and armed with a warrant, two Charleston detectives and two patrolmen entered the James Island condominium of one Mr. Jerry Shields, Cybersecurity Manager for Mercy General Hospital. He had just returned from a late dinner with his girlfriend, and ten minutes later, found himself handcuffed and locked in the back of a squad car.

Allen and Sarah were stunned when they learned it was Shields and not Blake Fitzgerald who was part of the drug scam. It turned out Fitzgerald wasn't a criminal, but as Angela had said, "Just an asshole."

The real shocker came several weeks later. Davis's wife, Sherry, was convinced her husband's declining health didn't make sense. Chris had always been the picture of health. He worked out, didn't drink too much, and watched what he ate. She knew that sometimes these things just happened, but not to her Chris. She tried on multiple occasions to involve the police, but the department said there wasn't anything they could do.

Ben Barnett, a detective from the Charleston Police Department, was friends with Chris Davis, and Sherry convinced him to look into the matter. Most of his investigation was done on his own time, so it took a while for him to make any headway, but once he gained access to Chris' medical records and discovered the presence of oxalate crystals in his kidneys, he convinced his captain to open a formal investigation. As soon as it became apparent that Chris may not be able to return to his job at Mercy, the personal items from his office were boxed and sent home to his wife. On a hunch, Detective Barnett sent the contents to forensics, and that's when traces of ethylene glycol were discovered in his office coffee cup.

The focus of the investigation now centered on the employees working in and around the purchasing department. Barnett hit pay dirt when he discovered that a 32-ounce bottle of high purity ethylene glycol had been ordered from the Alliance Chemical Company and delivered to the Goose Creek home of Miss Kate Parker. The shipment was delivered around the time Davis began to display his symptoms.

An analysis of Miss Parker's financial records uncovered not only the second mortgage on her home, but an additional loan, plus substantial balances owed on her credit cards. Kate Parker was so far underground with her debts, she was breathing dirt. She was taken into custody, and a warrant was issued to search her house and car. Cocaine residue was found in both locations. She confessed to her growing dependency on the white powder and a proclivity for fine jewelry. She had been working in the purchasing department at Mercy General longer than any other employee and was livid when she was once again passed over in favor of Davis for the manager's position. She tried to convince the cops she had no idea the ethylene glycol would make him that sick. She only wanted the job she was entitled to, and the attendant $20,000 pay increase. No one was buying it. She was booked and charged with attempted murder with the promise of a first-degree murder charge should Davis die.

Amy continued to juggle The Cup and college, stealing precious moments with Nick when their hectic schedules allowed. She would soon complete her last semester of classroom work, and was thrilled to learn she'd be doing her student teaching at Daniel Island Elementary School. Nick surprised her with a weekend trip to the farm in Killian. Nick's dad and Amy hit it off famously that weekend, with Robert making Amy promise she'd come back as soon as she and Nick could get away again.

Life was slowly returning to what might be called normal as the weeks passed and the temperature cooled. Fall and its glorious weather had once again returned to Charleston.

EPILOGUE

IT WAS THE second week in November when the six new dogs completed their training and were picked up by a TSA representative. Homeland Security was pleased with the results and immediately promised Nick an order for a second batch of sniffers.

The whole crew was out at the Academy the following Sunday afternoon to celebrate the new order. The keg was tapped and the wine opened when Nick called everyone to the office for another announcement.

Nick had noticed Isaiah's old bike was about to fall apart, so he found one on Craigslist equipped with a small electric motor and told everyone what a great job Isaiah was doing and how important he was to the business. Isaiah was beaming when Zach rolled out the new bike and started explaining how it worked.

Allen had brought Sarah and her husband, Dave, to the party, and Josh was giving them both a tour. Sally, Amy, and Angela were busy getting the food ready, and Nick was working the grill.

Allen smiled to himself and realized how lucky he was to have found these people. They'd all been there for him when he needed their help—he may not have survived without them. A few weeks before, he'd received his company's $25,000 fee from MediGroup along with a hand-written note from Jack Rennells with the words "Above and beyond." Attached to the note was an additional check for $25,000.

Allen met with his lawyer and J.P. Morgan Investment Banker to create a trust fund entitled, "The Opioid Fund," with an initial funding of $50,000. The first fund payment would be in the amount of $25,000 and issued to the "MUSC Center for Drug Addiction and Treatment Research."

A short time later, Nick announced the hamburgers and hot dogs were ready. Sally was busy dishing out the food when Nick noticed Allen on the phone in what looked like a serious conversation. When he hung up, he joined Nick by the keg.

"What was that all about?" Nick asked, handing Allen a beer.

"Interesting call from someone who needs some help with a problem."

"Great, good luck with that."

"Well, it may require the additional services of someone with a bit of canine law enforcement experience." Allen smiled. "Know anybody that might be interested?"

Nick shook his head and said, "Oh shit, here we go again!"

Another Nick Giordano novel
Coming in 2018

THE TOOLS OF THE TRADE

CHAPTER ONE

He looked like a lawyer. Wearing one of his many $3,000 virgin wool Armani suits, Phillip Bryson was pushing fifty—his jet-black hair showing only a touch of gray. At a shade over six feet tall, he carried himself in a manner that displayed a sense of confidence and privilege. Bryson's driver pulled the black Cadillac Escalade to the curb in front of Antonio's Bar at the corner of Bay and Erie in Jersey City. He snapped shut the Bosca attaché resting next to him, leaned forward, and said, "Thank you, Isaac, I should only be about twenty minutes."

~~~~

Phillip Bryson's parents, Christian and Olivia Bryson, were the quintessential New York City power couple from the 1970s through the early 2000s. His father was a nationally-known
~~~~

corporate attorney, and his mother was the fashion editor at the New York Times. Their son had been groomed from a young age to carry on the family's legacy of power. After graduating from Harvard Law School in 1989, Bryson joined the U.S. Attorney's Office for the Southern District of New York, which encompasses the boroughs of Manhattan and the Bronx in New York City, along with several outlying counties. While he could have demanded a salary four to five times what the government paid if he had joined one of the city's major law firms, Bryson saw the U.S. Attorney's Office as the fastest path to make a name for himself in the pillars of power—and he did just that. He spent the next twelve years cultivating his contacts while prosecuting white collar crime and public corruption cases. He rose rapidly within the political bureaucracy of the department. An impressive string of major convictions brought Bryson a national reputation as a relentless prosecutor. Despite his relatively young age, there were rumblings he was being considered for the Assistant U.S. Attorney General's position in the Justice Department.

In an unsuspected move, he left the U.S. Attorney's Office in 2001, partnering with two fellow attorneys to start the Bryson, Hilliard, and Swanson Law Firm. The new firm was headquartered in New York City, and quickly became known for its aggressive defense of high profile individual and corporate clients. His years of tenure and contacts cultivated at the Attorney's Office were now paying dividends just as he had planned. Phillip Bryson had entered the highly lucrative gray area of the law where—for a price—individuals and their organizations were protected by the same statues designed to protect the innocent—despite the fact that many of them were anything but innocent.

A few years after leaving the Attorney's Office, Bryson was approached by an individual by the name of Mr. Smith who represented an investor who wished to remain anonymous. The investor wanted Phillip to personally handle a major real estate deal. Real estate transactions of this magnitude in the city are always challenging and require extremely meticulous negotiations. Impressed with the professional manner in which Phillip managed the deal, his firm was given a substantial amount of additional legal work by this unnamed benefactor.

About a year later, Phillip was relaxing in his Greenwich Village condo on a Sunday morning, when he received a phone call from Mr. Smith. He was told that a car was waiting outside his building that would take him to a meeting concerning a special situation requiring his legal assistance. As Bryson exited his building he saw Smith standing next to a black limousine parked at the curb. The tinted window made it impossible for him to see inside. Smith smiled and opened the rear door—an obvious invitation for him to get in. He did.

Phillip slid into the back seat and found himself seated next to a man that looked to be in his sixties. The inside of the car was dark, and it took a moment for Bryson's eyes to adjust. The man wore a camel hair sport coat over a black dress shirt, its collar open. He looked to be fairly short but in good shape for his age. His dark complexion accentuated the full head of silver hair combed straight back. His face showed the beginnings of a five o'clock shadow even though it was still mid-morning.

As the limo pulled away from the curve, the man turned to Phillip and said, "Mr. Bryson, I wanted to thank you personally for the good work you and your firm have done on behalf of some of my operations."

"Thank you, sir. We appreciate the opportunity." Now that his eyes had adjusted to the light, Bryson did not have to ask the name of the man sitting next to him. Mario Rossini had been a fixture in New York and New Jersey's underworld for decades. He oversaw several business enterprises, some of which were legitimate, but many were said to be linked to the Genovese crime family, one of the "Five Families" that dominate organized crime activities in New York City and New Jersey.

Rossini had never been one to waste time on pleasantries. "I'd like you to deal with a situation that's come up. There's a lawyer over at the U.S. Attorney's Office making noise about charging one of my associates with tax fraud. These charges are obviously false, but they need to be dealt with none the less. I'd like you to personally handle this for me. I'm assuming you have good friends over at the Attorney's Office that might just reconsider going forward with any actions against my associate if they knew you were personally involved in the matter. I'd consider this a personal favor. Mr. Smith will give you the specifics."

"Thank you, Mr. Rossini. I'll look into it."

"I'm sure you will." The limousine came to an abrupt stop at the curb in front of Bryson's office building. Mr. Smith was waiting, and after opening the rear door, Phillip got out. The rear window slid down, and Mario Rossini said, "Enjoy the rest of your day, Phillip."

Smith and Bryson stood at the curb and watched the limo pull into traffic and disappear down Broad Street. Mr. Smith gestured toward the entrance to Bryson's building and said, "Shall we?"

Smith left an hour later. Phillip sat at his living room staring at a manila folder in front of him. The folder outlining the criminal charges being considered against a Mr. Samuel McGrath, Chief Financial Officer of Cumberland Salvage and Recycling. It didn't take long for Phillip to realize Mr. McGrath was salvaging and recycling money for Mr. Rossini's business operations— salvaging and recycling as in money laundering. Phillip walked to the window and gazed out over the Hudson River. He was coming to grips with the enormity of the decision he was about to make. He realized that if he went ahead with Rossini's request, there would be no going back.

The next morning, he dialed the number of an old friend at the U.S. Attorney's Office. The phone was answered and he said, "Charlie, I hear you're handling that business with Sam McGrath over at Cumberland. I need a favor."

Over the next few years, Bryson found that more and more of his time was being spent on the legal affairs of Mr. Rossini and his associates. Eventually, he was forced to shed his other clients and devote the entirety of his time to handling the ever-increasing demands of the Rossini account.

Each year Phillip Bryson's partners were becoming more concerned with the firm's association with Rossini's organization and its purported ties to organized crime. Finally, in 2005, the partners gave Bryson an ultimatum—resign the Rossini account or resign from the firm. The demand didn't surprise Phillip; he was only surprised their demand had not come sooner. He also knew that there would be no way that Mario Rossini would ever let him walk away. He simply knew too much. After the ultimatum was given, Phillip stood, smiled at each of his partners, removed a piece of paper from his suitcoat breast pocket, and said, "Gentlemen, my letter of resignation. I wish you well." He placed the letter on the table in front of him and calmly left the boardroom. Phillip Bryson was now the private attorney for Mario Rossini and would become even more entangled with its inter-workings and secrets of his organization. He had finally crossed over to the dark side.

~~~~

The exterior of Antonio's looked like a typical small neighborhood bar with its nondescript exterior painted charcoal-gray. It was a two-story building with the main bar on the ground floor and a small social club above it.

Bryson exited the Escalade and entered the bar, pausing for a moment to allow his eyes to adjust to the dim light. The inside of Antonio's was actually quite nice, with a long, polished mahogany bar complete with brass foot rails. A large backlit mirror with three rows of liquor bottles ran against the left wall behind the bar. Two men sat at the bar nursing their drinks, seemingly to take no notice of Bryson. It was clear they were both packing. There was an open area in the rear of the bar containing eight tables covered with red-checkered tablecloths and wine bottle candles. The place had a comfortable feel to it.

Bryson nodded to the rather rotund, gray-haired bartender. The bartender returned the nod indicating he was expected upstairs. Phillip headed directly to the rear staircase which led to the second floor housing its own small bar, several large leather chairs and sofas, and a sixty-inch flat-screen TV mounted on one of the walls. Mario Rossini and Salvatore "Sal" Ruggiero were seated in chairs watching CNN. As soon as Bryson entered the room, Ruggiero, the younger of the two men, grabbed the remote and shut off the flat-screen. In the hierarchy of organized crime,
~~~~

Sal Ruggiero is what's called a capo, or caporegime, and reported directly to Mario Rossini, known as one of the organization's underbosses. Rossini was responsible for the family's business operations in the Southeast part of the country and reported directly to the head of the Genovese family, Liborio "Barney" Bellomo.

Rossini had just been booked on racketeering charges under the RICO statute. His arraignment had been held last week, and he was out on bail. The judge had set dates for the preliminary hearing, pre-trial motions, and trial. Bryson took one of the chairs across from the men and said, "I met with one of my contacts in the U.S. Attorney's office, and he gave me a heads-up on what they've got so far. He also let me know they think they might be able to connect you directly to Charleston. They're still gathering evidence from people down there."

Mario Rossini asked, "What do they have?"

"Mostly circumstantial evidence concerning your operations and any association with Genovese's people," answered Bryson. "I'm concerned with what they may uncover in Charleston. As you know, they've got Angelo Vitale in a federal prison down there. Do you know if he could connect you to Charleston?"

"No," answered Rossini. "DiMarco ran the operation down there with Grasso, and they've both been removed from the equation. Vitale was just a soldier."

Ruggiero added, "They got Vitale in solitary, so we can't get to him like DiMarco."

Bryson turned to Rossini and asked, "Anyone left in your Charleston organization outside of Vitale that might cause problems?"

Even though the question was directed to Rossini, Sal Ruggiero answered, "The whole fucking thing is a piece of shit. The good news is that DiMarco and Grasso were the only real ties to Mario, and they're both dead. I'm moving Frank Petrelli in from Atlanta to reorganize and salvage what we can down there. We'll be cleaning the money out of Orlando until things settle down. Once that—"

Phillip Bryson raised both hands interrupting Ruggiero. "Sal, I don't want to know your plans. My only concern is how to legally protect Mario and his businesses. The less I know about the specifics the better. Now, my question was a simple one. Do you know of anyone that could testify as to specific acts that took place in Charleston that could be directly connected to Mr. Rossini?"

Sal Ruggiero's nostrils flared—he didn't abide to being lectured to. It took a moment for him to compose himself before answering, "I was getting to that before you interrupted me. Like Mario said, DiMarco and Grasso were the only two who had any direct contact. And like I said, they're both dead. There's no doubt Vitale knows our businesses down there, but he never had any direct contact with Mario. But, we still may have a problem."

Now it was Rossini who spoke, "What problem?"

"All right, I've got some special friends inside the Charleston police department," Ruggiero said. "DiMarco had set up a minor operation involving taking narcotics from a hospital and a few urgent care places down there. My guy thinks someone at the hospital got suspicious and hired a computer guy named Allen Miller. This Miller guy hacked in to their computers and figured out what was going on. Vitale tried to scare him off, but it didn't work. Finally, Grasso and Vitale snatched Miller and were trying to find out what he knew when some of his friends showed up. That's when Grasso and one of his men were killed, and the cops arrested DiMarco and Vitale. The Feds threatened them with a shitload of RICO charges, including murder. The assholes caved and agreed to testify against Mario. I told you DiMarco has been taken care of, and Vitale is probably no real threat."

Mr. Rossini asked, "So, what do Miller and his friends know?"

Ruggiero replied, "According to my contact, the Feds took over. Local cops are out of the picture now, but my guy did give me some information."

"And that was?" asked Bryson.

"Miller worked for the government doing some kind of classified cybersecurity work before he got to Charleston. The cops think his secretary and a few of his friends got involved in busting up DiMarco's hospital thing and exposed some of our other operations down there."

"Names?" asked Bryson.

Sal removed a small notepad from his pocket and opened it. After flipping through the pages, he said, "Secretary's name is Sarah Pryor. There's also a guy that runs a dog training business named Nick Giordano and two guys working for him. The two guys are ex-Army, but I didn't get their names."

"Sal," Rossini said, "get ahold of your cop contact. I need to know how much this Miller guy really knows and if he can connect any of it to me. Same goes for his secretary and the dog guy."

Bryson stood, "Gentlemen, I believe this is a good time for me to leave. Mario, I'll let you know as soon as I have more on this." Bryson nodded at Ruggiero and left the room.

Mr. Rossini waited until Bryson left and the door was shut, "Sal, these people might need to be taken care of. You got someone to send down to Charleston to handle that?"

Ruggiero thought for a moment, nodded, and said, "Carlo Tucci."

ABOUT THE AUTHOR

Geoff holds graduate degrees in business and education. After a successful career in advertising and financial relations, he taught elementary school. Teaching became a passion, especially teaching reading and writing to his young students. That passion turned to writing both children's stories and adult mystery novels. He lives in Charleston, SC with his wife, Sally. He has three grown children, Max, Leigh, and KC and two sets of twin grandchildren; Collin and John and Lily and Cora.

OTHER BOOKS BY
GEOFF AND ART COLLINS

NIKKI AND THE TREE KEEPER

 *"What a wonderful and lovely tale!"*

 *"Nikki is a heart-warming and inspirational story of finding your place in the world."*

 *"Nikki and the Tree Keeper is magical."*

 *"The illustrations are beautiful and add so much to the book."*

www.nikkiandthetreekeeper.com

THE CHRISTMAS TOKEN

⭐⭐⭐⭐⭐ *"The Christmas Token is a heart-warming holiday tale about generosity, memories, and family."*

⭐⭐⭐⭐⭐ *"The artwork in this tender story is superior!"*

⭐⭐⭐⭐⭐ *"The Christmas Token should become a family tradition to read as the Christmas season begins!"*

⭐⭐⭐⭐⭐ *"Excellent!"*

⭐⭐⭐⭐⭐ *"Lovely book! My kids have read it many times over the holidays."*

www.thechrislmastoken.com

THE ADVENTURES OF ARCHIBALD & JOCKABEB

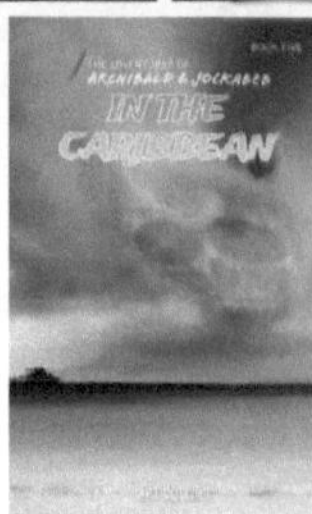

 **"One of a kind!"**

This is the best book EVER!!!!!! Dragons, Indians, horses, evil crows, there is nothing like it! I loved it…can't wait for more adventures to come.

 **"A majestic tale -Harry Potter meets The Indian in the Cupboard"**

Loved reading these books. I quickly got hooked, dug in, and engaged with the characters. Wonderful stories."

 **"Rich in vocabulary!"**

This book is rich in vocabulary. I can't wait to read all the other Archibald and Jockabeb books!

 **"Best of the best!"**

In the Forest is an outstanding book! The characters are great and help make the wonderful story come together.

 **"Terrific series of action books!"**

www.theajadventures.com

WHITE CLOUD AND THE GOLDEN CANYON

 *Excellent Native American tale for children and adults alike.*

 *Wonderful life lessons for all.*

 *Very enjoyable and true to our culture. (Akta Lakota Museum)*

www.whitecloudandthegoldencanyon.com

Coming in 2018...

THE BLACK CREEK MYSTERIES

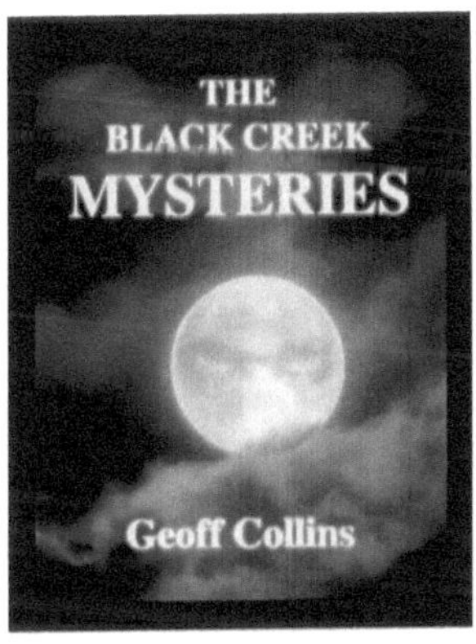

Alex Foster and Travis Sanders live in a small Southern Ohio farm town named Rivers Edge. Their first adventure takes them to the remote desert town of Sunshine, Arizona, where they find themselves in the middle of the Legend of the Apache Death Cave. The following summer, Alex and Travis have just graduated from high school and are headed to the small fishing town of Black Creek, Maine for a relaxing vacation before they both head off to college. Their trip becomes anything but relaxing, when they discover a mysterious underwater cave and a network of deadly gunrunners.

For more information, visit www.booksbycollins.com

Reading Partners is a nonprofit literacy organization that recruits and trains community volunteers to provide one-on-one reading tutoring to students in under-resourced schools across the country. This highly-effective program has helped thousands of children master the fundamental reading skills they need to succeed in school and beyond.

For more information, please visit www.readingpartners.org

"Literacy is not a luxury; it is a right and a responsibility. If our world is to meet the challenges of the twenty-first century we must harness the energy and creativity of all our citizens."

—President Bill Clinton

www.ingramcontent.com/pod-product-compliance
Lightning Source LLC
Chambersburg PA
CBHW030024200726
48283CB00012B/848